OUR

WILD

WEEKEND

MAMMOTH

A book for Vanessa

First published in Great Britain 1986
by Methuen Children's Books Ltd
Published 1990 by Mammoth
an imprint of Mandarin paperbacks
Michelin House, 81 Fulham Road, London SW3 6RB

Mandarin is an imprint of the Octopus Publishing Group

ISBN 0 7497 0321 0
A CIP catalogue record for this title is available from the
British Library
Printed in Great Britain by
Cox & Wyman Ltd, Reading

ONE

My name is James Espie and this is about the Albert Memorial trip to Murtagh Bay, organised by Mr Fisher and Edwina Greenfield, but mostly by Edwina, because old Trout is past it.

The first thing that happened was that Trout got us lost on the way to Murtagh House, where we were supposed to be staying.

There are miles of paths, winding through the sea buck-thorn and the sandhills from the Arches Bridge where the South Eastern Board minibus left us off, but Trout didn't stick to them.

'Everybody quiet! Listen to the bird song!' he said, shushing us, and then he hopped off up a sandhill, gripping his pipe between his teeth.

Sixteen weary Memorialites and Edwina trudged up after him, lugging our holiday gear.

'Perhaps Miss Greenfield can confirm the presence of a dunnock?' Trout burbled.

A dunnock is a bird, in case you didn't know. We can't help knowing because Trout is master in charge of the whole Lower School, and he is always on about them. We do Bird Surveys and Migration Charts and we have a Bird Spotters' Competition that I don't enter for.

Edwina didn't tell us whether Trout had heard a dunnock or not. She wasn't looking pleased. I think Edwina had worked out that we should have stuck to the marked path, which would have taken us to Murtagh

House straight away.

We went on for miles and miles under the merciless sun. My Dad says Edwina Greenfield has the loveliest bottom in the world ... my Mum says the Espies are only at the Memorial so that he can come and admire it on Parents' Day ... and Edwina just marched on, wiggling it about in her blue jeans. I bet it was watching Edwina wiggle that made Trout lose his sense of direction.

Then old Doris Speed got over-heated, and my sister Phyllis told Edwina, and Edwina shouted to Trout that we would have to stop to let Doris cool off. It was absolutely typical Doris. There is a lot of Doris, and when she sat down she fairly flattened the sedge grass. Doris is a Natural Disaster for anything she sits on.

'Sir! Sir!' Phyllis sang out.

'What is it, Phyllis?' Trout asked, trying to look as if he hadn't noticed Edwina taking his map to see where we were.

'Are we lost, sir?' Phyllis asked.

That is just like Phyllis. She has no idea when to keep her mouth shut. Trout opened his mouth to snap her head off, and Phyllis got offside by hiding behind Beaky who was sitting on his rucksack looking puffed. Serve him right for bringing a rucksack, which he only did to show off. He had on a red and white knitted hat, with *Brian Brian Brian* written round it. His name is Brian Thornton, but we all call him Beaky because of his nose.

'Take off your cardigan, Doris,' said Edwina, spreading Trout's map out on the sand.

'I don't want to, Miss,' said Doris, who was red in the face and practically had steam coming from her ears.

'Well, really!' said Trout. Edwina had squatted down beside Doris, and was talking to her. Edwina gave Trout a dirty look. Old Doris getting over-heated was all his fault. Trout was supposed to be in charge of things, but we all knew that Edwina was the one we had to look out for. The trip was Trout's swan song before he retired to where ever Trouts retire to.

'I suggest we all rest for a while,' said Edwina, standing up. She hadn't made Doris take off her cardigan, and that was a surprise. Edwina took the map over to Trout, and they started talking about it.

I got Noel and Norrie while everybody was thinking about giving Doris the kiss of life, and we decided that we would go off to see the sea.

'We can hear it, so it can't be far!' I told them.

We juked off between the sandhills, and came out on a flat bit of turf, studded with blue flowers, little tiny ones. It was a valley about forty metres across, with the sandhills and buckthorn all around it, and lots of little paths and windblows leading off it. We followed the sound of the waves in and out between the dunes and round the buckthorn and over a last hill, and there it was.

'Isn't that beach big?' Norrie said, in awe.

It was the biggest beach I have ever seen, stretching for kilometres and kilometres and kilometres, with great big rollers pounding in.

'Great!' said Noel.

We ran right down to the tide line, and got some stones and chucked them. Then the tide got Norrie's C&A bag, and soaked all his things.

'Sod that!' said Norrie.

'Should have left it further back,' said Noel.

'I know that,' said Norrie. 'But I didn't, did I?'

'We'd better get back,' Noel said. 'If they spot that we're missing, Edwina will have our guts for garters!'

'I wouldn't mind being a garter on Edwina,' said Norrie.

'Neither would Trout!' I said. 'We should be going back.' Noel repeated. 'Doris has probably revived, and we don't want them missing us.' Trust Noel. He is always the one who gets nervous first.

We started back and were only just in time because Trout was getting everybody organised. Edwina had worked out where we were, and she had taken over the map.

We started off, and Phyllis came up to me.

'Old Beaky got done again,' she said.

'Okay. What happened?' I said.

'They made him eat sand,' she said. 'Dennis Ray and Sprout and Buns.'

I wasn't surprised. That is just like Dennis and his mates. They are all in the Chess Club, and they have a kind of Chess Club Gang.

'It was horrible,' Phyllis said. 'They stuffed his head down in it, and then Carol poured some water on him, and they kept saying he'd wet himself.'

'Big joke,' I said.

'Where did they get the water?' Noel asked.

'Beaky had a water bottle in his rucksack,' said Phyllis. 'They took it off him, and they knocked off his glasses and they wouldn't stop it when we told them to.'

'What do you want me to do about it?' I said. 'I'm in enough trouble already with the yogurt.'

I made this yogurt trap for old Carol. She got the yogurt down her leg and she bawled about it and Trout did his nut. He was on about sending me home because of it, and the fag. It was Norrie's ceremonial fag that he doesn't smoke and I got caught with it.

'Nothing,' said Phyllis. 'There's nothing you can do, is

there?'

'Let's go and see Beaky,' I said, feeling a bit uncomfortable.

'Leave him,' said Norrie. 'It's none of our business if he gets in fights and wets himself.'

'He didn't wet himself,' said Phyllis.

Norrie opened his mouth to say something, but then he shut it again. There was nothing we could say, and nothing much we could do, either. Dennis is about six times bigger than anybody else in our class, and he goes *wild* when he wants to. He doesn't care who he hits, or where.

'Somebody should tell on Dennis,' Phyllis said.

'Yeh, well, that's up to Beaky, isn't it?' Norrie said.

We all knew why Beaky wouldn't tell. He wouldn't tell because he'd only get done later, and worse. The Chess Club are like that.

We got to Murtagh House and there was a big hairy man waiting for us. He was called Bernard. He was the Warden, and he had an equally big dog that sniffed Doris.

'You all right, Beaky?' I asked.

'Yeh,' Beaky said.

He had put on his anorak, to hide the place on his pants where Carol had poured the water. Carol is Dennis' girl friend, sort of.

'You keep out of his way,' I said, meaning out of Dennis' way. 'Otherwise you'll be his packed lunch for the weekend.'

'I know that,' Beaky said.

We all put our things in Murtagh House, and then Edwina said to hurry up and we would go down on the shore and have our First Night Barbecue.

We reckoned it would be great.

TWO

There was a place for barbecues down on the beach, with logs laid out round it, and the ground all blackened in the middle.

'Right, kids!' Edwina said. 'Fuel hunt commence!'

We split up, and headed for the drift wood and the bushes.

Dennis Ray came up to me, which wasn't a big surprise.

'I want a word with you, Espie,' he said.

'Oh yeh?' I said.

'You cleared off down to the beach, earlier,' he said. 'You don't clear of anywhere any more without my permission, see?'

'Who says?' Norrie asked.

'Trout says,' said Dennis, with a grin. 'Trout says I'm the eldest and I'm to look after the little ones. He said I was to keep an extra special eye on you, Espie, because of your mucking about. You *and* your teeny weeny mates.'

Trust Trout! Anybody else would have known who the cause of all the trouble was, but not Trout. Telling Dennis to look after everybody would have been funny, if it hadn't been mad.

'We're as old as you are,' Norrie said. 'Well, almost.'

'You're not bossing us around,' said little Noel.

'*Oh great*!' I thought. '*Thanks a million, Noel*.'

What did he have to come over brave for? Noel is normally the one who hides at the back. This time he was hidden at the back all right – he was standing furthest away from Dennis – but he was volunteering Norrie and me for the high jump.

'Do you want trouble, then, Espie?' Dennis said. I reckoned I was the one he was mainly after.

'I don't have to go around fighting people, Dennis,' I said. 'I'm not dumb.'

'You just do what you're told, and we'll get on all right,' Dennis said. 'Be a good little boy.'

He was egging me on to lose my temper, so that he would have a good excuse for clobbering me. I wasn't going to give him the chance. Getting Dennis would take a Great Espie Plan, if not a miracle, and just then I hadn't had time to think of one.

'You're yellow, Espie,' Dennis said, and he went off back to Sprout and Buns.

'You shouldn't have let him call you yellow,' said Norrie. 'You're almost as big as he is.'

'Now he'll keep after you,' said Noel.

'You were quite right not to fight him, James,' said Lorna Wallace. She'd come up in the middle of it.

'Scrub off, Wallace!' said Norrie. 'This is our business.'

'Charming!' said Lorna and she went off down the beach to her sister, Charlotte.

'If you're so keen to tackle Dennis, do it yourself!' I told Norrie.

'Dennis could stuff both of you,' said Noel. He was probably right, even if we had been able to get Dennis on his own to try it out. But the Chess Club aren't like that. They're all big, and they stick together, Dennis and Sprout Wright and Buns Boyle.

'Old Trout must be balmy!' Norrie said.

'Ga-ga,' I said.

'Past it,' said Noel.

We were still going on about Dennis when we got our wood back to the fire, and piled it on. Trout lit up. At first it wouldn't burn, but then it did, and the flames billowed right up the air, and it was great!

We had sausages and Doris Speed burnt her thumb and Edwina told her to suck it, which is nothing new for Doris. Then Trout made an announcement.

'Attention all!' he said. 'Time for races!'

'Races!' Norrie muttered.

We were disgusted! You would think we were kids or something. Trout wanted to make a big thing of it, a kind of Murtagh Bay Olympics, and he started us off with his whistle and stuck Doris down at the far end with a rope. The rope had Noel on the other end of it and the idea was that they would hold it up like a tape and then we would burst through it and be winners.

We had our race, and Dennis burst through the rope, and then Doris pulled it up again, and the three behind Dennis got tangled in it, and the whole race ended in a pile.

Beaky came up to me.

'I didn't wet myself,' he said.

'I know,' I said.

'They're saying I did, but they poured water over me, that's all,' said Beaky. 'Down my trousers, so it would look like that.'

He stood there with his silly hat on, looking at me.

'Why me?' he asked.

'They've plenty of people to pick on in school.' I said. 'But there's only a few of us on the trip, right? And nobody who is bigger than Dennis. I expect we'll all get our turn.'

'Yeh,' he said. It seemed to cheer him up, making him think we were all in the same boat.

'Just be crafty and stay out of Dennis' way,' I said. 'Right?'

'Right, James,' he said.

I seemed to be everybody's choice for Leader of the Opposition against Dennis, which I could have done without. I mean, at school *I* stay out of his way, and I wouldn't have come on the trip if I'd known who was going to be on it. Usually, there's people from the upper forms, and if they'd been there Dennis couldn't have done his act, but old Trout had had to cut down on his numbers at the last moment, and that was how we wound up with Dennis thinking he was running things.

Beaky pulled his hat down over his ears and went off to find some shells for Edwina. I don't know if Edwina *wanted* shells, but Beaky kept trotting back to the fire and showing them to her and saying how beautiful the colours were.

You have to be pretty stupid to talk like that to a teacher, even Edwina.

Edwina was looking great. You could see why Trout fancied her. It was beginning to get dark, and she was bent over by the fire and she had the top two buttons of her blouse undone.

'Phew!' said Buns. 'Look at that!'

Edwina was bending down and I think she heard him. She gave him a dirty look.

'If you had kept your mouth shut we would have seen more!' Norrie told him.

'Wait'll she goes swimming!' Buns said.

We all thought about it.

'Yabba-dabba-do!' Norrie said. 'I wouldn't mind going swimming with Edwina!'

Noel walked off.

'What's the matter with him?' Sprout asked.
Then Buns started shouting after Noel.
'*Boyle*?' said Edwina.
She'd crept up on us!
Maybe she hadn't. I don't suppose Edwina could be bothered creeping up on a bunch of kids. What matters is that she heard what Buns was saying, and she didn't look pleased.
'Yes, Miss?' said Buns, going beetroot and wriggling about.
'*No*, Miss!' said Edwina, sharply.
She looked at us.
'I'm pretending I didn't hear what I just heard, right?'
'Yes, Miss,' we said.
'But I don't want to hear what I'm pretending I didn't hear another time! Understood?' She went away.
'Reckon you won't be getting off with Edwina this trip,' I said.
'Reckon you won't either,' said Sprout. 'You'll have to stick to kissy-kissy with old Lorna.'
He went off.
'What's all this about Lorna Wallace?' Norrie said.
'Nothing,' I said. I didn't know about Lorna. Maybe she *did* fancy me. Great!
I went off to join Noel. He was down by the edge of the water, looking at it. It was coming in fast, with little ripples, and you had to jump back to stop it getting you.
'It comes in fast because of the channel,' I told Noel. The sandhills where Murtagh House stands are where the sea used to be, but there is a kind of lagoon, called the Inner Bay, and the beach is split by a wide channel leading down it. Trout told us it had taken centuries for the sandhills to form and make a lagoon of the Inner Bay, and

he said he would show us new ones forming. He says the sandhills are always shifting.

There was a bang-bang-bang sound then, like a distant popping.

'What's that?' Noel asked.

'It's the Army,' I said.

'I don't see any Army.'

'The other side of the channel. Kinleer Camp. There's a firing range.'

'Do you think they could hit us, standing here?' Noel said.

I wasn't sure. We couldn't see the camp at all, because it was a long way away, hidden amongst the sandhills on the other side, but we could see the red light for the helicopters coming in, and they had red flags as well, to warn people who didn't know that the sandbanks were a firing range.

'That side is the Army camp,' I told Noel. 'This side is the Nature Reserve.'

'So long as they don't get mixed up,' Noel said.

I knew what he meant. We were supposed to be getting away from soldiers and things, playing hunt-the-dunnock, and there we were with guns going pop-pop-pop just across the way.

'You'd think they could do their shooting somewhere else,' Noel said.

I was still wondering about Lorna, so I thought I'd tcst it out on him.

'What do you think of Lorna Wallace?' I asked.

'She's all right,' Noel said.

'Do you think she fancies me?' I said.

'Do you fancy her?' he asked.

I did. Well, I didn't. It was complicated. I mean, there

isn't much of that stuff really going on at the Memorial, only lots of talking about it.

'She's not too bad,' I said.

'I think she probably does fancy you,' Noel said, sounding very serious.

'You reckon?'

'Yeh.'

'Great!' I said.

'What about Dennis?' Noel said.

'I bet Lorna doesn't fancy him,' I said.

'Old Carol does, though,' said Noel. 'It's not who fancies him I'm talking about. It is what are we going to do about him?'

'Nothing,' I said. 'Just keep out of his way till the weekend's over. He'll soon forget about us once he gets back to school.'

'Dennis told Carol he was going to get you,' said Noel. 'She told Waldo Milligan, and Waldo told me.'

'I'll look after Dennis,' I said, although I still didn't have a clue how I was going to do it.

'Come on you lot, time for bed!' Trout yelled.

Time for bed!

You would think we were little kids. Maybe we were, in his mind. Trout has been taking little kids on trips since the wheel was invented. He doesn't know that things have changed. I don't *mind* Trout. The only thing that is wrong with him is that he makes you feel like a kid, all the time, when you're not.

It is a real put-off.

THREE

Murtagh House was great upstairs.

There was a Boy's End and Girls' End with Teachers' Rooms in between to keep them apart.

'Not just to keep us apart,' Phillis pointed out. 'Trout's door is right opposite the top of the stairs, so that no one can creep down without being spotted.'

'What do you want to creep down for?' Doris asked.

'For the Last Night,' Phillis said. 'Haven't you ever been on a Trip before? Everybody breaks out on the Last Night.'

'Are we supposed to?' asked Doris, nervously. She is big and pink, and not great breaking out material.

'Of course we're not supposed to,' said Phillis. 'That's why we do it!'

'How are we going to break out?' I asked.

'I don't know yet,' said Phyllis. 'But we are. We'll save up food and have a Midnight Swim and a Feast and then we'll break back in again and Trout and Edwina will never know.'

The trouble with Phyllis is that she reads too many crummy books about girls at boarding schools breaking out of dorms and things.

'A Midnight Swim mightn't be *safe*,' said Noel.

'We'll swim where it *is* safe,' said Phyllis. 'If it is safe by day, it ought to be safe by night.'

'In the daytime people can see you if you get in trouble,' Noel said.

I thought Noel was right. Trout takes us to the Leisure Centre and we do Safety Lessons and one of them is about not going swimming on strange beaches without proper supervision. I told Phyllis, and I added: 'Also there's the current. You should have seen the water rippling in the channel when the tide was coming in.'

'You're scared,' Phyllis said.

'I'm not scared,' I said. 'Just sensible.'

'Okay then,' said Phyllis. 'We'll break out on the last night and have a Midnight *Paddle* and a Feast. Satisfied?'

'If you are sure it is safe,' said Doris, tugging at the arms of her cardigan. It is a big woolly pink one that makes her look like an elephant.

'Everybody in bed!' Trout howled, coming up the stairs, and we all split off down the corridor to our rooms.

I was in Room 3 at the Boys' End with Noel and Norrie and Beaky. We were pleased because we'd been kept clear of the Horrors' Room, which had Dennis and Buns and Sprout and Waldo Milligan in it.

'I like it here,' Beaky said, bouncing on his bed.

'Just so long as you don't get in our way!' Norrie said.

'Lay off him, Norrie,' I said.

'Okay,' said Norrie.

We all got into bed, and Trout came along and turned off the light.

'Goodnight, boys,' he said.

'Goodnight, Sir,' we said.

We heard his footsteps going back down the corridor to his room, and then the sound of the door shutting.

'... eighteen, nineteen, twenty!' I said, giving him a count to settle, and then I nipped out of bed and put the light on.

'What did you put the light on for?' Beaky asked,

blinking.

'Because we want it on,' said Norrie. '*See*?'

'Okay,' Beaky said, and he got out a book and started reading it. It was a bird book.

'Look at him!' groaned Norrie.

'There isn't much to look at!' I said.

Norrie got out of bed and whipped Beaky's *Brian Brian Brian* hat which had been sitting on his rucksack.

'What are you doing with that?' Beaky asked. 'Give it here.'

He got up out of bed.

Norrie had gone over to the sink, and he was running the tap.

'Give me my hat!' said Beaky.

'I'm going to wash it,' said Norrie. 'Phew! It's a stink-eroo. It looks as if it needs washing.'

'Give it to me,' said Beaky.

'Oh, give it to him, Norrie,' I said. Anybody else but Beaky would have grabbed the hat from Norrie and stuffed his head under the tap, but Beaky didn't. He stood there, looking trembly, and shouting about getting his hat back.

'Shut up, Beaky,' Noel said. 'Somebody'll hear you.'

Norrie dropped the hat into the basin.

'It floats!' he said.

'Give over, Norrie,' I said, uneasily.

'Let's see if it submarines!' said Norrie, and he put his hand in the water on top of the hat, and pressed it down.

Beaky went scarlet. He lunged across the room and grabbed at the hat, but Norrie pulled it out of the water and dodged him.

'Want your hat?' Norrie said.

'You give it to me!' said Beaky, looking as if he was

going to burst into tears.

Norrie gave it to him ... *right in the chops*!

SPLATT!

Beaky stood there gulping, with water dripping down on his pyjamas.

'Ha, ha! Got you!' said Norrie.

'You shouldn't have done that, Norrie,' Noel said.

'You all right, Beakyman?' I asked Beaky.

Beaky took his hat over to the sink, and tried to wring it out. When he'd finished he hung it on the window latch to dry, and then he went back to bed.

'That got him!' Norrie said.

Beaky put his head under the clothes.

He lay there, a hump in the blankets, with his rotten bird book closed on the pillow, where he'd dropped it.

'I wish Dennis wasn't here,' Noel said, suddenly.

'Why?'

'He isn't so bad at school, where there are lots of people to fight, and lots of people to stop him,' Noel said. 'It is going to be different here.'

'Dennis won't pick on us if we stick together,' said Noel.

'Oh great,' I said. 'Who is he going to pick on then?'

'Probably *you*,' said Norrie.

'We'll stick together!' said Noel. 'We'll make a pact. The whole room will stick together, and then none of us will get bashed.'

'What about *him*?' Norrie said.

I knew who he meant. So did Noel. Old Beaky couldn't stick up for himself, let alone anybody else.

'It is the whole room, or nothing,' I said. 'Agreed?'

'Agreed!' said Norrie.

'Agreed!' said Noel.

The hump in the bed didn't say anything. He didn't even

move. I expect he didn't feel like saying he'd stick up for us after the way Norrie had done him.

'He's asleep,' I said, but I didn't think he was.

'You shouldn't have done that to his hat, Norrie,' Noel said.

'You should apologise,' I said.

'Why?' said Norrie.

'Because if you do things like that you're no better than Dennis,' Noel said.

'Only a lot smaller,' I said.

There was a knock at the door, and Edwina's voice sounded through it.

'Lights out in there, James!' she said, crisply.

We'd reckoned we would be able to hear Trout trouticling along the corridors, and that Edwina would stick to the girls' end, but she had foxed us with her fairy footsteps. Trust Edwina. She is about three times as bright as Trout, even if he is Head of Lower School, and she is only a new teacher. Trout thought that he was going to be Headmaster when the old Head went, but he didn't get the job, the new Head got it instead. We reckoned that that was one reason why old Trout was chucking his job in and going to the Great Trout Pond in the sky. The other was that Trout is *senile*, almost! He would have made a *naff* Headmaster.

'And no more racket, James.' Edwina said through the door. *Me... again*!

Norrie got out of bed and put the light off, and we heard her going down the corridor.

'... Eighteen, nineteen, twenty!' I counted. 'Will I switch on?'

'No,' said Norrie.

'Leave it till she's safely gone to bed,' said Noel.

'All right,' I said.

We lay there in the darkness.

Boom-boom-boom went the Army guns.

'Reckon they're having a night practice,' I said, and I went over to the window and pulled the curtains back, to see if we could make out any gun flashes.

'If we were the I.R.A. we could swim across and blow them up and swim away again,' said Norrie. 'Like "The Guns of Navarone".'

'That was cliffs,' said Noel. 'They had to go up cliffs.'

Pretty soon the boom-boom-boom stopped, but I didn't get to sleep. I lay there listening to all the little sounds I couldn't hear before, and one particular one, the sound of the waves on the far beach, where the channel met the bay.

I listened to the sea, and I thought about old Beaky, humped up in the bed opposite, with his head under the clothes.

I should have stopped Norrie.

I *could* have stopped Norrie, I suppose. He's big, but he's not that tough. Not as tough as he'd like to be, as tough as Dennis and the others.

They all take it out on Beaky. Beaky is a natural target, with his funny hat and his rucksack and some of the daft things he does.

I was glad I wasn't like Beaky, and glad I wasn't like Dennis either, which brought the thought back ... I hadn't done anything to stop things happening to Beaky.

I *could* have, I *should* have, but I hadn't.

I stopped thinking about it. I thought about Lorna Wallace instead, and that was nice.

FOUR

Lorna was sitting on the low stone wall in front of Murtagh House.

'Hi,' I said.

'Hullo, James,' she said.

She has big eyes and long black hair.

'When's breakfast?' I said.

'Dunno,' she said.

'Neither do I,' I said.

The dialogue was really g-r-e-a-t. I was trying to think of something to say like, 'Do you fancy me?' or something brilliant like that when Phyllis bounced up.

'We found a way out!' Phyllis said.

'Out of what?' said Lorna.

'Out of our room,' said Phyllis. 'For the Last Night and Midnight Swim ...'

'Paddle,' I said, interrupting her.

'Paddling is for kids,' she said. 'Anyway, I said I'd find a secret way out, and I have, and it is absolutely Top Secret and nobody else is going to be able to find it, because it is in our room.'

'What is it?' I said. 'A fire escape, or something?'

I knew Doris and Phyllis had the little room, round the bend at the end of the corridor. The girls' end had two big rooms and one little room, and as usual Phyllis had managed to get herself the best pitch. Doris was in it with her because Doris is her best friend.

'There's a trap door in our room,' said Phyllis. 'It leads

up into the roof space. We waited until Edwina had gone, and we got some steps from the cupboard in the hall. I went up them and opened the trap door, and got into the roof space. It is a great big place, like a Cathedral, and you can walk along the joists. Half way along there's a door and I went through it. There's a platform with some sort of weather thing on it, and leading down from the platform there's a ladder which takes you onto the roof of the stables, and you can get off onto the yard wall and you are out!'

'Brilliant!' I said.

'Terrif!' said Noel, who'd turned up in the middle of it. 'How do you get back in again?'

Trust Noel to think he'd get locked out, just as soon as we'd discovered a way to escape from Edwina and Trout's little kids' bedtime.

'The same way you got out!' said Phyllis. 'Honestly, Noel, if Doris can do it, anybody can!'

She was right. Doris is no acrobat.

'How did you get old Doris through the trap door?' I asked.

'No problem,' said Phyllis.

'It must be some trap door,' said Noel.

Lorna hadn't said anything. She was sitting there fiddling with a little ring she had on.

'Great, isn't it Lorna?' I said.

'Yeh,' she said.

Edwina came down the steps from the house, and stretched. It was lovely!

Old Noel nearly fell off the wall!

'Good morning, everybody,' Edwina said.

'Good morning, Miss,' we said.

'Everybody sleep well?' Edwina asked.

'Great, Miss!' said Noel.

'Smashing,' I said. 'Except for the boom-booms.'

Edwina made a face.

'They don't seem to be firing guns this morning, Phyllis said.

'Good,' said Edwina. Then she asked me to go and see when our breakfast would be ready, and she stayed out in the front, talking to Phyllis and Lorna.

Trout had come out to the front, and he had taken over Edwina. He was muttering a lot, and sucking his pipe.

'Hung-over!' I said.

'What?' said Noel.

'Secret drinking parties in the Teachers' Rooms with Edwina!' I said.

'I bet Edwina doesn't drink,' said Noel. 'Only milk.'

'She drinks gin and brandy and vodka by the trillion!' I told him.

'You're making it up,' Noel said.

I know the trouble with Noel. He is in love with Edwina, but he doesn't want anybody else to notice until he has Plighted his Troth.

Everybody is in love with Edwina, except Dennis and Buns and Sprout who only lust after her Lovely Body, and they are too thick to be considered.

'Breakfast in twenty minutes, Miss,' I said.

'Good,' she said. 'I'm famished.'

'Just time for a brisk walk!' said Trout, remembering he had come to take us all into the great open spaces. 'Come along children.'

Lorna had gone. I thought about going after her but Edwina spotted me, so I didn't get the chance.

Off we went with Trout spouting about the formation of the sand dunes and the threat of the sea buckthorn. He went on about it so long that we were late back for our cornflakes.

After breakfast, Trout lined us all up again, and marched us off into the blazing sun.

Trout made us into a crocodile, two by two. I got Norrie. Lorna was at the back, with her sister Charlotte.

It wasn't nature this time. It was Stone Age Man.

Trout had got Bernard to mark some Stone Age cooking sites on his map of the reserve, and the idea was that Trout would lead us to them.

'Bet he gets us lost,' Norrie said to me, and of course he did.

Carol got sand in her eye and Edwina stayed behind washing it out of her and then Sprout ran off into the bushes shouting that he had to go somewhere quick and Doris hurt her ankle in a rabbit hole. I hope there wasn't a rabbit in it.

'All right!' said Trout in exasperation 'Half an hour break, then reassemble here!'

Off went the Memorialites, heading over the sandhills for the sea, which we'd just about been able to spot through the dunes. It was all bright and glittery with the sunlight winking on the surface.

'That's beautiful!' said Beaky.

Then Buns came up to him.

'Hold out your hand,' he said.

'What for?' old Beaky said.

'Just hold it out,' he said.

He pressed something into Beaky's hand.

Old Beaky went really green.

'What's up?' I said.

It was a piece of paper, cut in a circle, all squiggled over.

'The Black Spot,' said Buns.

I got it.

We'd been doing *Treasure Island* with Edwina in School.

'It means *he's* for it!' said Buns, and off he went.

'It's not fair!' Beaky said.

'What's going on?' Phyllis said, arriving beside us.

I told her.

'He might get really hurt if Dennis starts into him,' I said.

'I'll tell,' said Phyllis, coming to a decision.

'No, you won't,' I said.

'Why not?'

'Because it wouldn't make any difference. Dennis would find a way of getting him anyway.'

'It's all right for you,' Beaky said, bitterly.

'I'm on your side,' I said. 'So's Noel and Norrie!' And I told him about our pact. 'You would have been in it, only you were pretending to be asleep,' I added.

'You and Norrie and Noel, against Buns and Sprout and Dennis?' said Phyllis.

'And Beaky,' I said.

'You'll get mashed,' Phyllis said. She sounded worried.

'Maybe we won't,' I said. 'Maybe we can think of something.'

'I could tell them I'm going to tell, without actually telling,' suggested Phyllis.

'He'd get you as well,' Beaky said, glumly.

'He likes getting girls,' I said. 'He enjoys people saying he's a bully. That's his image.'

Trout started yelling for us all to form up again in a crocodile.

We did but when we got back into line I found that

Phyllis had worked a swopsy with Norrie.

'You can't take on the three of them, James,' she said. 'The Chess Club will murder you!'

She was really frightened.

'Don't try it, James,' she said.

FIVE

The next thing that happened was at lunch.

There were two tables, and I was at Edwina's.

'Enjoying yourselves?' she said.

'Yes, Miss,' said everybody.

'Great fun, isn't it?'

'Yes, Miss.'

'I hope you are learning a lot?'

'Yes, Miss.'

Honestly, there are times when Edwina is as bad as Trout. I felt like saying: 'No Miss. It's rotten, Miss. We're all bored stiff, Miss, and when are you going swimming?' We all reckoned it would be good when Edwina went swimming, but so far no one had even mentioned it.

I thought 'Why not?' so I said:

'Miss?'

'Yes, James?'

'When are we going swimming, Miss?'

'Probably after the Castle, James,' she said.

'Yabba-dabba-do!' Norrie said. Norrie isn't very original.

'Are *you* going swimming, Miss?' Waldo Milligan said. Trust Waldo to ask it right out!

'Wait and see!' said Edwina.

That's what we all intended doing!

Carol Coulter passed me a note. It said:

J. ESPIE IS A DIRTY THING.

'What for?' I said, looking down the table at her.

'You know fine well!' Carol said. She hadn't forgiven me for squirting the yogurt on her leg on the bus.

I would have flicked some of my rice pud at her but I had finished it, so I flicked some of Norrie's instead.

It got her right on the glasses.

'I'll get you for that, James Espie!' she shouted.

'Carol? James?' Edwina had wakened up.

We didn't say anything.

'What's that on your glasses, Carol?' Edwina said.

Carol took off her glasses.

'Rice pud, Miss,' she said, and she wiped them on the table cloth.

'*Carol*!'

'Oh, sorry Miss!' Carol said.

'Well, *really*!' Edwina said. 'Now James, are you in any way connected to this rice pudding?'

'Or part thereof!' Noel muttered.

'Connected?' I said. Connected means 'Joined on to.' I wasn't joined on to the rice pudding on Carol's glasses or the rice pudding on the table cloth, I wasn't even near them. I was nearer the rest of the rice pudding on Norrie's dish, but as that was just disappearing into Norrie it didn't count in the calculation.

'No, Miss,' I said.

'Have you at any time been connected to it, James?' asked Edwina.

That is the trouble with Edwina. She knows me.

'Yes, Miss,' I said.

'How, Miss?' said Edwina. She was taking the Mickey out of me by saying 'Miss' like that.

'Flicked it, Miss,' I said.

'Flicked it?' said Edwina. 'Why?'

'Flicked it at Carol, Miss,' I said.

'I know who you flicked it at, James. That wasn't my question. I want to know *why* you flicked it at Carol?'

Old Carol was grinning like mad. I could feel myself going red. I didn't want Edwina to see the note because then she would start asking what the note was about.

'Just,' I said.

'Just *what*?' said Edwina. 'Just*ice*, I suppose?'

'Yes, Miss,' I said.

'Espie's Revenge?' she said.

'Yes, Miss,' I said, brightening up a bit. 'Espie's Revenge' didn't sound bad. Maybe I was going to get away with it.

'Revenge for *what*, James?' she asked, icily.

Some of the girls started to giggle. I couldn't see what Lorna was doing. Perhaps it was just as well.

'Well, James?'

'Nothing, Miss,' I said.

Trout woke up from his doze, and came fussing over, too late as usual.

'Trouble, Miss Greenfield?' he said. He was doing his Knight-in-shining-armour-and-damsel bit, only it wasn't Edwina who was in distress, just me.

'It's only James,' Edwina said.

'Espie,' said Trout.

'Yes, Sir.'

'Well, Espie?'

'Sorry, Sir,' I said.

'See me afterwards,' he said, and he went back to his table.

'There you are now, James,' said Edwina, and she went back to her rice pud.

Old Carol sent me another note. It said:

HA-HA. SERVE YOU RIGHT!

'Finished, everyone?' Trout said. 'Right! Assemble in twenty minutes for the Castle Trip.'

'What about swimming, Sir?' Norrie asked.

'Oh yes, bring your swimming gear, those of you who want to swim.'

The big question was whether Edwina would bring hers.

We all queued up to get out of the door.

Sprout got on one side of me, and Buns got on the other.

'You shouldn't have mucked old Carol.' Buns said.

'Dennis will ruin you!' Sprout added.

Buns jogged me.

'Chicken, Espie?' he said.

'No, *rice*!' I said. It wasn't even funny.

Somebody tweaked my hair.

'Ouch!' I said, spinning round.

It was Dennis.

Trout bore down on us.

'We'll see you later, Espie,' Buns muttered, and they moved off.

Trout gave me a real tongue lashing. I was yes-sirring and no-sirring like mad! He went on and on, and then he said I'd better apologise to Miss Greenfield as well, and he took me to apologise to Edwina.

Edwina was in her room.

We knocked on the door, and she came out of it fiddling with her bra strap, only it wasn't her bra strap it was the strap of her bathing costume which she had slipped on underneath her clothes. So she *was* going swimming! I bet Old Trout's eyes were bulging!

'Espie has come to apologise for the incident at the dinner table, Miss Greenfield,' said Trout.

'Sorry, Miss,' I said.

'That's quite all right, James,' she said.

'It's not quite all right with me!' said Trout, grimly 'I think you understand that, don't you? This time Last Warning means Last Warning, any more trouble, and home you go.'

'I'm sure James will be a good boy,' Edwina said.

Then she patted me on the head.

Honestly!

You would think I was some little kid who had wet his nappy or something. I was really mad.

'Off you go and get your swimming things, James,' said Edwina.

I beetled off.

'Edwina's swimming!' I told Norrie and Noel.

'So what?' said Noel.

'SO-HO! said Norrie, and he started doing a wiggle, but Trout came out to count us and he had to stop.

'Sir?' Phyllis said.

'Yes, Phyllis?'

'Sir, could we please not go in crocodiles this time because it is boring,' Phyllis said.

Trust her!

I didn't like crocodiles because they made us look like little kids. Almost no other teacher in the world makes us go in crocodiles, but Trout does. The thing was that this time I *wanted* to be in a crocodile, because in a crocodile I could keep clear of Buns and Sprout and Dennis.

'No,' said Trout.

'Oh Sir, why?'

'*Because*,' said Trout.

'You'd think we were little kids!' said Phyllis, when he was out of earshot.

'You are!' said Dennis. He'd come up behind us, with his Champion Kid Smasher look on.

'Dry up, Dennis,' I said.

'You needn't think I've forgotten about you, Espie,' he said. 'You're on my list, with Beaky.'

Still, at least I didn't get him in the crocodile. Norrie got Noel, and I got Beaky Thornton, which meant it was going to be a long walk.

SIX

'My little legs are dropping off!' Noel said to me, pitching down on the grass beside the stump of wall.

We'd been going up and down the towers in Drumrath Castle so that Trout could show us the view and explain how Drumrath commanded all the sea approaches to that bit of Down.

'I've scraped my knees, too!' Noel said, and he insisted on showing us the cut he'd got when Sprout pushed him. They were right up on the battlements and Noel said he thought he was going to be dashed to death on the rocks below, but I don't think there was much danger. It was when the pushing and shoving started that Edwina made Trout bring us down.

'You boys are no use anywhere!' Phyllis told us.

'Boys are hopeless!' said Charlotte Wallace who was with her. Lorna is her sister, but you wouldn't know it. Charlotte Wallace is a pudding. 'Especially Noel Smith!' she added, just to complete Noel's day.

'It wasn't my fault,' Noel said, when they'd gone off.

'Who cares?' I said.

'I'm fed up getting in trouble,' Noel said.

'Trout's threatening to send me home on an Ulsterbus,' I said.

'He won't,' said Noel.

'How do you know he won't?'

'Because he'd have to refund your trip money if he did, and he's spent it all on drink!' said Norrie, pitching himself down on the grass between us.

'And tobacco for his pipe,' said Noel.

We all thought it might be true.

You can tell when Trout is coming by the puffs of smoke. When he's *not* at school, that is. The new Head doesn't allow him to smoke his pipe at school, and Phyllis thinks that is the reason he gets so cross. The old Head didn't mind.

Phyllis came up.

'Still unbashed?' she said.

'Dennis won't pick fights here,' I said. 'Too many teachers about.'

'Where is Dennis anyway?' asked Doris, flopping down on the grass and killing trillions of grasshoppers. She started picking daisies and decorating the sleeves of her cardigan with them.

'Don't know and don't care,' I said.

I'd seen something moving down by the moat. It was Carol. She came up the side of it, very flushed.

Dennis came out of the trees, behind her. Carol didn't turn her head when he shouted at her. She kept on going.

'Somebody's had a row!' Phyllis said.

'Carol should have known better than to go in the moat with him,' I said. There wasn't any water in the moat, just trees and bushes and a lot of cover.

'She's really keen on Dennis, old Carol is,' said Phyllis.

'*Was*,' I said, looking at Carol. She was over by the wall, sniffing into her hanky. Charlotte Wallace had gone over to her, and Charlotte was doing all the talking.

Edwina and Beaky came walking across the grass towards us. Beaky was wearing his snorkel round his neck. He'd been carrying it all the way from Murtagh House, trailing round and round after Edwina up inside the castle keep. It was typical Beaky.

'Time for a swim?' Edwina said.

'Oh yes, Miss!' everybody said, and we all got up.

'You swimming, Miss?' Norrie said, trying to make it sound casual.

'I wouldn't mind a dip at all, Norrie,' Edwina said, and she went off with Beaky to round up the others.

'Yabba-dabba-do!' said Norrie. I wish he would think of something else to say. It is dead boring.

'You're just a spotty kid, Norrie,' said Phyllis, scornfully.

'Yeh!' muttered Doris.

'You think it is great to talk dirty. Well, it isn't, so there.'

'Naff off, droopy drawers!' said Norrie.

'Naff off yourself!' said Phyllis.

'Come on!' I said. 'Drop it! We've got more important things to do.'

The castle was on a big hill, with a road leading down from it to the Main Street, and the harbour where the coal boats came in. We all went down the hill, with Edwina leading the way, clutching her towel under her arm. Charlotte Wallace was behind her, walking beside Carol and Lorna. Carol was in the middle, and they were all talking.

'Look at that!' said Norrie. 'Old Carol is hot stuff.'

'Shut up or Trout will hear you,' I said.

Dennis and Buns and Sprout were further back. They'd got hold of Beaky, and they were jostling him, threatening to put him over the ditch. Sprout got hold of his snorkel, and started trying to take the table tennis ball out.

If Beaky had been sensible like the rest of us he would have come up and got offside, sticking close to Trout, but he didn't.

We came down into the Main Street, just opposite the

harbour, and everybody wanted to go into the shop and get drinks, so we did.

'Hi, Jessie James!' Sprout said, pushing past me.

'Staying close to teacher today, aren't we?' said Buns.

'I wonder if Jessie can swim?' said Dennis.

Sprout had Beaky's snorkel stuffed up inside his shirt, and old Beaky was after him, arguing.

'We ought to tell on him,' Phyllis said. 'It isn't fair. He never picks on anyone his own size.'

'Who doesn't?' said Doris.

'Dennis doesn't,' said Phyllis.

'It's Sprout who has the snorkel,' said Doris.

'Doesn't matter, same thing! You bet if one of us went in and tried to get the snorkel off Sprout to give it back to Beaky – what would happen? Dennis would happen, that's what! Dennis would be flying around punching people.'

'Telling wouldn't do any good,' said Noel, glumly.

'What about an anonymous note?' said Phyllis. 'We could get together and write a note telling what Dennis is doing and then he'd get hammered for it by the teachers and he wouldn't know who'd told on him.'

'I bet he would,' said Noel.

'It wouldn't matter if he got *expelled*, would it?' Phyllis said. 'If he was expelled we would be all right.'

'You might be,' said Noel. 'I wouldn't. He lives up our way. He'd get me.'

'Anyway, people don't get expelled for just anything,' I said. 'You have to burn down the school or rape the teachers or something.'

'Don't talk dirty, James,' Doris said.

'What did I say?'

'I'm not saying it,' said Doris. 'You said it, and you know what you said.'

'I was trying to have a sensible discussion about whether people can be expelled,' I said. 'If you are too much of a kid to listen to words like r-a-p-e then you should go home and play with your dollies.'

'Why do all boys talk dirty all the time?' Doris wanted to know.

'Makes them feel like big men,' said Phyllis. 'Some hopes!'

'Girls don't talk dirty,' said Doris.

'I think Doris is right,' said Noel.

'Good for you, Noel,' said Phyllis.

'This is dead boring,' I said. 'Can't we talk about something else?'

'Yes,' said Norrie. 'S-E-X!'

'No,' said Doris.

'Double no,' said Phyllis.

'Treble no,' I said. 'Shut up talking smutty, Norrie, or naff off somewhere and take a peek at page 3.'

'I don't need to,' said Norrie. 'I'm going to have a peek at Edwina instead!'

Old Phyllis looked disgusted. 'Come on Doris,' she said, and off they went to catch up Edwina.

'What did you have to say that for, stewhead?' I said. 'Now they're mad. Maybe they'll tell Edwina.'

'Well, we are,' said Norrie. 'I am, and you are, and Noel is too, only he won't say so. We've all been waiting for ages and ages for Edwina to strip off and hop around in her bathing suit. You know we have. Only nobody is honest about it except me. That's why I get blamed and you lot don't. If you were honest, you'd admit it!'

'Okay,' I said. 'I'm honest. I want to see Edwina ... but I don't spend all day going on about it.'

'I'm not fussed about Edwina,' said Noel.

'Yes, you are!'

'No, I'm not.'

'Liar,' I said. 'You know you are. Norrie's right.'

Noel's neck had gone red.

'Own up, Noel!' said Norrie.

'I'd *quite* like to see her,' Noel admitted.

'Then you are dirty minded, just like everybody else!' said Norrie, in triumph.

'I don't go on about it, though,' said Noel.

'What's the difference?'

'It's a big difference,' Noel said. 'If I want to see Edwina with her clothes off that is private and personal, see? Wanting to see Edwina with her clothes off is just a ... a sort of getting ready, that's all.'

'Getting randy, you mean,' said Norrie.

'No, I don't,' said Noel.

'Getting ready for *what*, then?' said Norrie.

'For being in love,' Noel said. 'For getting married and everything.'

'Oh *that*,' said Norrie.

'Yes, *that*,' said Noel.

'That's all rubbish,' said Norrie.

We came down to the harbour. The tide was in, and you could see the bottom. The water was clear, and deep.

'Girls change in the shed!' shouted Edwina. 'The boys can change round the back!'

'Yee-hoo!' shouted Norrie, and we dashed off to change.

It looked as if we were going to see Edwina in her bathing suit after all.

SEVEN

'She's not as big as I thought she'd be,' Norrie said.

'She's *great*,' I said.

Edwina was in her bathing suit. It was white, and had two bits, a top bit and a bottom bit, and it was tied together at the sides with little loops of cloth.

'Bet it comes off if she dives in!' Norrie said hopefully.

We were down in the water and Edwina was up above us, on the pier. She had brilliant legs and she had no bathing cap and so her hair was round her shoulders.

'It's lovely, Miss,' Phyllis shouted. She was splashing about down by the steps, with Charlotte Wallace.

'Come in, Miss,' said Charlotte.

'Coming,' said Edwina.

Then she held onto her nose and jumped in. If she had been in a James Bond film she would have done a swallow dive and we would have seen her lovely body arching above us, but as it was she nearly drowned Beaky.

She came up to the surface, and let go of her nose.

'Gosh, Miss!' said Beaky.

'Sorry, Brian,' she said.

Then she hitched up the top of her costume.

Edwina swam away to the steps, where she started persuading Doris to come in. Doris was standing there in her bathing suit, with her cardigan on, sticking her toe in and saying she didn't know whether she would go in or not.

'Ten minutes, everyone!' Trout sang out, from the end of the pier. He was sitting there, nursing his pipe. He wasn't going to let us see his wizened old legs.

'Race you to that boat, James!' Norrie said.

I raced him, and I won.

Then I raced Sprout and Waldo, and Waldo won.

'Give us your snorkel, Beaky,' I said, and Beaky did.

I had a go with the snorkel, but I didn't think much of it because all you could do was float around on the top with your head stuck under.

Then Norrie and Noel and I had a diving down competition. We were duck diving on the surface, and then we had to see who could swim nearest to Phyllis.

'Leggo!' she said, when I caught her leg. 'Oh, it's you.'

'Who did you think it was?' I said.

'Somebody *presentable*,' she said. 'Why don't you duck dive Lorna?'

Dennis shoved Carol in. She came down *kersplatt* and she was really upset about it.

'Dennis?' she shouted. 'I'll kill you for that!' She was all gulpy looking, and I thought she was going to burst into tears.

Charlotte and Phyllis and Lorna were floating on their backs. Norrie and I joined them.

'Why isn't old Doris swimming?' I asked Lorna.

'I expect she doesn't want to,' Lorna said.

Doris was up on the pier, talking to Trout and Trout was letting her use his glasses and they were watching some birds dive, out in the channel.

'Give us a tow, Norrie,' Phyllis said, and Norrie did. I gave Lorna one, only I sort of side-kicked her leg.

'Hey!' she said. '*Brute*!'

'Sorry,' I said.

'I'll probably bruise,' she said, and we looked for her bruise, but we couldn't find it.

Waldo did a dive.

He tried to show off and touch his toes, and he came down splat in a belly flopper.

'Ouch!' he said, when he came back up again. 'That hurt!'

'Serve you right!' Lorna said.

Then Dennis did a dive.

It was a good dive.

He went off higher up the steps than Waldo did. I tried one off the fifth step, and I almost banged my nose on the bottom, and Edwina told me it was because I wasn't turning my hands up when I hit the water.

'Do a dive and show us, Miss,' Sprout said.

'Not today, Colin,' she said.

'Why not, Miss?'

She didn't say and she didn't do one. She did another jump in, holding her nose. It wasn't very glamorous.

'She's afraid her bra will break if she dives,' said Norrie.

'Dry up,' I said.

'Why?'

'You know why,' I said, and I ducked under and swam off to the boat. I was fed up with Norrie, because all he wanted to do was talk about Edwina taking her clothes off. He'd got his mind stuck on it. I can understand anyone being stuck on Edwina but I didn't want to talk about it all the time. Thinking about it was enough.

Lorna and Charlotte were at the boat.

'Where's Phyllis?' I asked Lorna.

'Phyllis?' said Lorna. 'I dunno.'

From the way she said it, I thought she did know. Maybe Phyllis had gone off with Carol. I couldn't see weepy old Carol either.

'Come on,' I said. 'Where is she?'

'What do you want Phyllis for?' Charlotte said. 'She's your sister.'

'So what?' I said.

'So that's not much use, is it?' Charlotte said.

'She's all right,' I said.

'Please yourself!' said Charlotte, and then she and Lorna got into the water, and swam back toward the pier.

'Chasing both of them now, Espie!' said Buns. He swam after the Wallaces, and he caught Charlotte and ducked her.

Trout blew his whistle, and we had to get out of the water.

'Hurry along now, boys!' Trout said.

'*Boys*,' I said, doing my Trout imitation when he'd gone round the back of the shed.

'You watch he doesn't hear you,' said Norrie, busily drying his hair on Beaky's shirt.

'Hi!' Beaky said, grabbing it off him.

'That's my towel!' Norrie shouted

'It's my shirt,' said Beaky.

Norrie shoved him, and Beaky suddenly stuck out his fist BANG.

He got Norrie straight on the nose. Norrie went over onto his back, and his head cracked down on the cobbles.

'Hey!' I said. 'Hey, Norrie!'

Norrie just lay there.

He didn't say anything. He was moaning. He put his hands to his nose, and curled his legs up, and rocked about.

'It's my shirt!' Beaky said, looking down at him.

'You've hurt him,' I said.

'I never,' said Beaky. Then he repeated, 'It's my shirt.'

Beaky's eyes were glistening, and he'd begun to shake.

He looked scared.

'Get Trout!' Dennis shouted. 'Somebody get Trout. He's hurt bad.'

Norrie was still moaning and rocking about, and there was blood all down the back of his hands, pouring out from his nose.

'It's just his nose,' Dennis said. 'Stand back and give him some air.'

I was trying to get Norrie's hands off his nose, but I couldn't do it. I put my hands on his head, and there was a stickiness there.

'It's his head too, Dennis,' I said.

Norrie groaned.

It was a sort of long breath, with a rattle in it.

'You're for it, Beaky!' Sprout said.

'I just shoved him,' Beaky said.

'You hit him!' I said.

'Dry up, all of you!' Dennis said. 'Did anybody get Trout?'

'GET TROUT!' I shouted, and I wondered about putting my towel under Norrie's head but Dennis said not to. I was afraid to lift his head because of the blood, and because his brains might spill out. Then Norrie would be dead, and Beaky would be up for killing him or manslaughter, or something.

Noel scarpered to get Trout.

Old Trout really blew his top!

He started shouting at everyone when he saw what had happened.

'I think we ought to get a doctor, Sir,' Dennis said.

'Nonsense!' said Trout.

'Dennis is right, Sir,' I said.

'Who did this? Who is responsible?' Trout demanded.

Then Edwina turned up. She came belting round the side of the building, half-dressed.

'Miss, Miss, Norrie's hurt,' I said.

Edwina got down on the ground beside Norrie. She took his pulse and she felt his jaw with her fingers.

'Give him the kiss of life, Miss,' Buns said.

'You dry up, Buns,' Dennis said. I thought old Dennis was going to lay another one out.

'Norrie?' Edwina said. 'Norrie?'

Norrie opened his eyes and looked at her.

'Are you all right, Norrie?' Edwina asked.

'Yemuss,' Norrie said. I think it was meant to be 'Yes, Miss' but the words weren't coming out right.

'All right, Norrie,' she said. 'Just lie there. I'm going to move your hand so that we can see the damage. Let me move your hand, dear.'

She moved his hand away from the front of his face and a big splatter of blood landed on her bathing costume. You could see the red all down her front.

'Give me something!' she said, waving her hand out behind her.

I gave her my hanky.

'That's *filthy*, James,' she said.

Dennis gave her his.

She started wiping Norrie's face, getting the blood off.

'Everybody keep back,' Dennis said. 'Give them room.'

We all got back, except Trout. He had stopped shouting now, and gone all jittery.

Dennis went up to him.

'You ought to sit down, Sir,' he said, and Trout did! I've never see anything like it.

'You've just had a fall, Norrie,' Edwina said. 'You're all right. You are all right, aren't you, Norrie?'

Norrie nodded.

'Fall?' said Trout, getting excited again. He got up on his feet, and started shouting at us again.

'Come on!' he demanded 'This is no time for nonsense.'

'It was an accident, Sir,' I said.

'What sort of an accident?' said Trout.

'Just mucking about, Sir,' I said. 'He fell, sort of.'

'You *again* Espie?' Trout said. 'I warned you, didn't I? If this boy is really hurt ...'

'It wasn't him, Sir,' said Dennis.

'It was me,' said Beaky.

Old Beaky was white as a sheet. He looked as if he was going to start bawling any minute.

'What was you?' said Trout.

'I ... I shoved him, Sir,' Beaky said.

'Thumped him,' somebody muttered.

'He had my shirt, Sir. He was mucking about with it. I sort of shoved him and he went back.'

'He banged his head, Sir,' I said. 'It wasn't Beaky *shoving* him, it was banging his head.'

'His head is cut,' said Edwina, who was still on the ground, fussing over Norrie. 'I think it is nothing serious, but there might be concussion. We ought to get him to hospital, just in case.'

Trout went off to telephone for an ambulance but before he got one Bernard turned up in his landrover with a doctor. Someone had told him there had been an accident.

'Round the front, boys, out of the doctor's way,' Edwina said, and we all herded off.

We gathered together at the front of the shed with Bernard and his dog, and the two teachers were round the back, where we'd been changing, with Norrie and the doctor.

Edwina came back and she said the doctor wanted Norrie to go to hospital for observation and she wanted one of us to come with her in Bernard's landrover so that Norrie would have a friend. She asked for volunteers.

'Me, Miss!' said Dennis.

'I want one of Norrie's friends,' she said, ignoring Dennis, who was shoving himself about to get attention. He'd been great when something needed doing, but now he was back to being Dennis-the-Menace again.

'James?' she said. 'What about you, James? Will you volunteer?'

'Yes, Miss,' I said.

Noel looked disappointed.

'Could Noel come too, Miss?' I said.

'Two is Company, Three is a Crowd!' Edwina said, deliberately trying to cheer us up and make light of it, but I could see that she was worried.

There were four of us, not two. Bernard was driving, I went in the front seat, Norrie got in the back with Edwina, and off we went to hospital.

EIGHT

I was in a pub with Edwina!

A *real* pub. Reas', in Downpatrick. It was great, with wooden seats and old advertisments for whiskey and a proper fire, although it wasn't lit because it was summer.

The pub was in the middle of Downpatrick and we were in it because the hospital said they wanted to keep Norrie for observation. Bernard had to go back to Drumrath as soon as he had dropped us off, and we were left waiting for the bus.

We went down to the bus station and there wasn't a bus for hours. Edwina got cross and said: 'Looks like we're stuck, James.'

'Yes, Miss,' I said.

'What are we going to do?' she said.

'Don't know, Miss,' I said.

'I'm a mess!' she said.

The trouble was that she had only been half changed when the alarm bells went about Noel. She'd put her jeans on but she hadn't brought her shirt. She had a cardigan on over the white top of her bathing suit, and the bathing suit was still covered in Norrie's nose bleed. The cardigan wouldn't button up properly because some of the buttons were missing, so she was walking around the middle of Downpatrick in a damp bathing suit covered with blood.

'You look all right, Miss,' I said.

'Flattery will get you fed, James!' she said, and she marched me off to Reas' pub.

My Mum and Dad don't take us in pubs. It was the first one I'd been in. I thought they would throw me out but Edwina said they wouldn't because we would go into the food part and have a meal, and we did.

Edwina had a Salmon Salad, and I had Sausage, Beans, Chips and *two* Cokes! Edwina had a brandy, because she said she was chilled inside after walking round with her costume on.

'Filled, James?' she said.

'Yes, Miss,' I said.

'We've still got half an hour to bus-time,' she said.

'Yes, Miss.'

'Best just to stay here, don't you think?'

'Yes, Miss,' I said. Then I thought I had better say something else or she would think I was dumb so I said: 'I suppose so, Miss.'

It wasn't *brilliant*. I mean it wasn't the kind of sparkling conversation you would expect from J. Espie dining tête-a-tête with lovely teachers, but at least it wasn't just: '*Yes, Miss.*'

'Well, James,' she said, but she didn't say well *what*. I think she was stuck as I was.

'It's a great pub, Miss,' I said.

'It is nice here, isn't it?' she said.

'Yes, Miss.'

'I'm sure Norrie will be all right,' she said. 'God I'm cold! I wish I could change out of this thing!'

She was nice. I don't think she'd thought about being still in her bathing suit until we got out of the hospital, and by that time she knew that Norrie was all right. She was really worried about Norrie, not just because she was Teacher-in-charge under Trout. I mean, it wasn't her fault that Norrie got hurt. She was looking after the girls. Trout should have been there supervising us, but he was pottering about at the end of the pier showing Doris to the herring gulls.

'You're very pale, Miss,' I said.

Usually, Edwina is a rosy colour. She has a cheerful face with red cheeks and she looks all bouncy; her smily face is one of the reasons why everyone fancies her. Now she was looking tired, though she still managed a smile.

'Yes,' she said.

I didn't know if I was supposed to be getting her something to drink. I was pretty sure they wouldn't let me buy anything but I would have offered, only I had hardly any money on me, about 40p, and I didn't think they would have any drinks Edwina would drink for 40p.

'I'm going to get some clothes!' she said. 'I can't sit around like this. Do you want to wait here, or will you come with me?'

'I'd better come with you,' I said, because I didn't want to be sitting in the pub on my own in case they realised I was there and threw me out because I wasn't eating. Edwina had said the only reason we could be in the pub was if we were eating, because I was under-age.

We went up the street, and Edwina stopped outside a clothes' shop. It was full of women's things.

'Are you coming in, or will you wait outside for me?' she said.

'I think I'd better wait outside,' I said.

'I'll just be a minute,' she said, and she went in. The door bell tinged behind her.

I was left looking in this window full of bras and knickers!

It was awful.

I went over the road, and stood outside the Grand

Cinema.

They were showing '10', and 'Confessions of a Window Cleaner.' I went to look in the window of the bookshop. It was full of books about religion and flower arranging and D.I.Y.

Edwina came out of the shop. She had a parcel under her arm, and she was wearing a white blouse.

'Like it?' she said.

'Yes, Miss,' I said.

'Almost bus time,' she said. 'Come on, let's go down to the station.'

'Yes, Miss,' I said.

We walked down a bit.

'Carry your parcel for you, Miss?' I said.

'Thank you, James,' she said.

She gave me her parcel. It was her bathing costume, I think. She must have changed out of it in the shop.

We had to wait for the bus when we got to the bus station. We sat on a seat in a really naff waiting room. She told me about Downpatrick Cathedral, which was up on a hill beside us.

'St Patrick is buried there,' I said. 'Three Saints Lie on Yonder Hill, Brigid, Patrick and Colmcille.'

'I know,' Edwina said.

I *knew* she knew, probably. I was only saying it to have something to talk about.

'My Dad took us up to the Grave,' I said.

'That's nice,' I said.

'Phyllis thinks it probably isn't his,' I said.

'Phyllis is a clever girl,' Edwina said.

'Don't tell her that, Miss,' I said. 'She has a big enough head already.'

Edwina laughed.

'Phyllis gets 'A's in everything,' I added.

'You don't do so badly yourself,' she said.

'I got three,' I said. 'The rest were 'B's and 'C's mostly.'

'You need to stop and think a bit, James,' she said. 'Things like the yogurt – there's been hundreds of things like that this term, James. Silly things, but you keep on doing them. Ever ask yourself why?'

I didn't answer.

'Strikes me you're acting all the time, James. Making up a person that you think will impress people. Lots of kids do that. Sometimes it doesn't matter, sometimes it can turn nasty. There are always going to be one or two people in any group who feel they have to chuck their weight about, picking on other people.'

That wasn't me, that was Dennis. Did she think it was me? I knew it wasn't, but I couldn't tell her that.

'Then there are odd bods, who have a difficult time,' she said.

'Like Brian Thornton?' I said, meaning Beaky.

'I don't want to discuss personalities with you,' she said. 'And anyway, I wasn't thinking so much of Brian. He's very strong inside. He'll get by, don't you worry.'

I didn't say anything. I wasn't impressed. Beaky is a sky-pilot, but she reckoned he was great!

'You seem to think you've got to *make* yourself special, James,' she said.

'I don't do that, Miss,' I said.

'Don't you?' she said.

She thought I did! She really and truly thought I did!

'I don't care whether people think I'm special or not!' I said.

'For someone who doesn't care, you work very hard at it, James,' she said.

The bus came in.

We got on, and Edwina bought the tickets to Drumrath.

We settled on the seat.

'You're going to be all right, James,' she said. 'You've a lot of imagination, and a lot of go in you ... but do drop the play acting.'

'Miss?' I said.

'Jesse James!' she said with a sudden grin. 'The Outlaw.'

She'd got it wrong. It was *'Jessie'* the chess club called me, like a big girl, not *'Jesse'* like the outlaw.

'Sometimes it's very funny, James, watching you. Like somebody in a comic, dashing about, jumping into things. But you can't go on being Jesse James forever. You need to sit still for a bit and think about who you really are, what sort of person you want to be. What you want to do with your life; what sort of job you'd like to have.'

'Lots of people haven't got jobs, Miss,' I said.

It was easy for her. Anybody looking at Edwina would give her a job. She could have been a Page 3 girl or a model or anything. Nobody was going to jump up and down crying 'Wow' when Jessie James unemployed came down to the Job Centre, were they?

'Yes,' she said. 'But it may not always be like this. Whatever about a job, and what you're going to be, it's time you thought about who you *are*, now.'

I couldn't make out whether she was mad with me, or not. I don't think she was.

'End of lesson,' she said. 'Right?'

I sat looking out of the window, not looking at her.

There was a big sign on the side of a barn.

It said:

WHATSOEVER things are TRUE,

WHATSOEVER things are HONEST,
WHATSOEVER things are JUST,
WHATSOEVER things are of GOOD REPORT;
If there be any VIRTUE,
And if there be any PRAISE,
THINK ON *THESE* THINGS.
Phillippians 4:8

Great!

A Personal Message to J. Espie, straight from God.

'Cheer up, James,' Edwina said. 'You're doing fine.'

'Yes, Miss,' I said.

Then I realised about the parcel.

It was sitting on the seat in the bus station! I'd left it behind me.

I told her.

'You silly boy,' she said, laughing. 'Don't get all upset about that! We'll ring the bus station, and I can pick it up tomorrow when I go for Norrie. It's only an old bathing costume, not the Crown Jewels.'

'I'm sorry, Miss,' I said.

'Never worry,' she said.

We got off the bus and Bernard was there with his landrover. He had promised he would meet the bus in case we were on it.

They got in the front of the landrover and I went in the back, and we drove out along the rough paths to Murtagh House.

Sprout was on the stairs when I got into the house.

'Hullo, *dear*,' he said.

'Buzz off, Sprout,' I said.

I could have hit him, but I didn't. I just went on up the stairs. He didn't know *anything*. She was really decent, and it wasn't me she called 'dear' it was Norrie, and that was only because he was hurt and she was afraid he was going to die.

Sprout can make *anything* sound ugly.

I was upset all of a sudden. Edwina had confused me. I didn't go into our room. I went to the Boys bogs instead, and I washed my face in cold water so that nobody would notice.

Then I took a good look at Jesse James in the mirror.

NINE

'What's that?' said Beaky, in the darkness.

I'd no idea he was awake. We'd been lying there with the lights out, and I was thinking about Norrie in hospital, and how he'd be getting on. Then the noise started.

'Rats?' said Noel, anxiously.

It sounded as if it could be rats. There was a lot of scraping and shuffling, but it wasn't coming from inside the room, or round the walls, it was coming from above us.

There was a muffled *Bang*!

I sat up.

'I've never heard of rats banging,' I said.

'Burglars?' said Noel.

Bang-bang-bang

Bang

Bang-bang-bang

Bang.

'Phyllis!' I said, scrambling out of bed.

'What?' said Beaky.

'I think it *might* be Phyllis,' I said, looking round for something I could bang back with.

Bang-bang-bang.

Bang.

Bang-bang-bang.

Bang.

'It IS Phyllis!' I said.

I knew it was because 3-1-3-1 is one of the Special Espie Codes we made up when we were kids. We used to bang on the wall between our rooms, and send messages that way. Phyllis was up in the roof space above us.

I chucked Beaky's rucksack off the chair, and then climbed up on the bed and banged the chair leg on the ceiling. I could just about reach, because we were up at the top of the house, and the ceiling wasn't very high.

Bang-bang-bang

Bang

Bang-bang-bang

Bang

I went with the chair leg.

There was a silence and then: *Bang*.

It *was* Phyllis, and we'd made contact.

'What's going on?' Beaky said, switching his flashlight on. Trust him to have a flashlight in his rucksack. 'What are you banging the ceiling for?'

'It's Top Secret,' I said.

'It won't be for long if you go on banging like that,' Beaky said, poking his pale nose up over the sheets.

'Look at that!'

Something appeared through the plaster. It was a pen knife blade, pushed down from above.

'She'll bring the ceiling down!' Noel said, anxiously.

'What's she doing?' Beaky asked.

The blade was sawing through the plaster. The dust drifted down in the torchbeam, like falling snow.

There was a cracking sound, and suddenly a square of plaster board was eased upwards, leaving a hole.

Phyllis' face peered down at us.

'Hi!' she whispered.

'Hi!' I said. There didn't seem much point in whispering after all the banging.

'What did you want to make a hole in our ceiling for?'

Beaky asked, gaping at her. He was astonished. We hadn't told him about Phyllis' escape route, because we didn't reckon he'd be Midnight Paddling on the Last Night.

'So you can go through it, stupid!' Phyllis answered. 'Anyway, I didn't cut a hole. There was a trap door here already, but somebody had covered it over with plaster-board. I've just gone round the edges, that's all. When we've finished with it, we can put it back in position, and it will cover the hole perfectly. Nobody will ever know.'

'Finished with it?' said Noel. 'What are we going to use it for?'

'For getting up here, of course,' said Phyllis. 'What else?'

'I *see*,' said Noel, doubtfully.

All we had to do was to take the mattress from Norrie's empty bed and put it on top of mine. Then we put the chair on top of the mattresses, and then we went up, one at a time. At least Noel and I did. Beaky held the chair for us, but he said he wasn't going up, no way.

'Okay,' I said. 'You stay and keep cavey for us.'

The roofspace was great. It was very high and all choked with dust and things. There were electric cables running along it, and we had to keep clear of them in case we electrocuted ourselves. We had to walk along the joists, and then we came to kind of walkway down the centre, and it led us to a little door.

'It is all right,' Phyllis said. 'It bolts on the inside.'

She found the bolt and shot it back.

We stepped out onto the weather gauge platform on top of Murtagh House.

'Phew!' Noel said.

It was brilliant!

We were right up high, and we could see a long way in

every direction, because the sandhills round the house weren't very big, and on the side that wasn't sandhills we could see the channel. We could see the harbour at Drumrath where Norrie got done, and the big blaze of light in the sky above the Army camp, and in the very far distance we could see Ballaghbeg, which is a town near Drumrath, looking very flat, with the Mourne Mountains rising straight up behind it.

'Let's go back in now,' said Noel.

'Shut up, Noel,' I said.

I wanted to go off into the sandhills, but Noel wouldn't go.

'It's too risky,' he said. 'I bet Edwina's still awake, and we're in enough trouble already.'

Apparently Trout had got really mad with them after we went off to the hospital and he said if there was any more trouble he would send for the bus to take everyone home in disgrace.

'Don't worry about Trout,' I said. 'He's always threatening to send people home. He never does it.'

'That's all you know,' said Noel.

'I bet Trout is busy filling Edwina up with brandy!' I said. 'I happen to know that Edwina drinks brandy. At least, that is what I got her when we were in the pub.'

I know I didn't get the brandy, but I wasn't going to tell them that. It sounded great.

'What were you doing in a pub with Edwina, James Espie?' Phyllis asked.

'I don't believe you were ever in a pub with Edwina!' Noel said.

Then I had to tell them all about it, including the sausage, chips and beans and the cokes and the bloodstains on Edwina, but leaving out the Jesse James bit because they might not get it.

'Then I left her bathing suit on the bus,' I said. 'So now she won't be bathing any more.'

'I bet she was pleased,' said Phyllis. 'If I were her I'd make you walk all the way to Downpatrick to get it!'

'Let's go back in,' said Noel. 'If we stay here we're risking getting caught.'

'I want to go down the ladder,' I said.

'And you're outvoted,' said Phyllis. 'It's my escape route, I found it, and I want it kept safe for the Last Night, so there!'

We went back.

Beaky had his nose stuck in the blankets. He was snoring.

'What a pig!' Noel said.

'Hold the chair,' I said.

'What for?' he said. 'You're not going up there again? You promised Phyllis you wouldn't, until the Last Night.'

'I've got to put the trap door back in position,' I said. 'Otherwise Trout and Edwina will spot it if they walk in here.'

It was a bit hairy balancing on the chair and trying to manoeuvre the trap door back into position, with my hands up through the hole, but I managed it, and clambered down again.

'That's fixed it,'I said.

'No, it hasn't,' said Noel, glumly. 'Look at it!'

The trap door fitted neatly into position, all right, but it was Phyllis' sawing that was the problem. The break in the plaster was a jagged one, and the shape of the trap door was clearly visible.

'Nobody will notice,' I said, hopefully.

'They will eventually,' Noel said. 'Bound to. Then we'll

get into trouble for damaging Trust Property.'

I thought about it. Phyllis should have been more careful. She had made a terrible mess. There was a lot of plaster on the floor as well.

'First clear this lot up,' I said.

I got a bit of cardboard and started putting the plaster flakes onto it and Noel got a sheet from his Nature Notebook and used it as a scoop to brush up the small bits. He used his handkerchief as a brush.

'What are you doing?' Beaky said, blinking at us from the bed. I don't think he had been asleep at all.

'What's it look like?' said Noel.

'That's the floor all right,' I said. 'What about the ceiling?'

We looked at it.

'Chewing gum,' I said. 'Tons and tons of chewing gum, stuck in the gaps. Then we stick paper over it.'

'Polyfilla,' said Beaky.

'And little strips of wallpaper,' I said. 'We'll stick it over the Polyfilla and paint it white.'

'Where do we get the Polyfilla and the wallpaper from?' Noel asked.

'We get the wallpaper from the bog, down behind the lavatory bowl where no one ever looks,' I said. 'We cut three centimetre wide strips off the wall, behind the bog bowl.'

'There are four sides of the trap door hole to cover,' Noel objected.

'There are five toilet bowls,' I said. 'We take a bit from each.'

'Okay,' he said. 'That's the wallpaper, if there's wall-paper in the toilet, and if it works. What about the Polyfilla and the paint?'

'There's some whitewash in the stable, in a bucket,' I said. 'We can use that. The ceiling is white, more or less. All we need is the Polyfilla.'

'Where do we buy that?' said Beaky, wide-eyed by this time, because he could see prospects of getting into trouble. The hole was in our room, and *he* was in our room, so there was no escape. Beaky never gets into trouble with teachers if he can avoid it.

'Maybe we could ask about the place?' said Noel.

'Oh yes,' I said. '"*Please, Bernard, we have made a hole in the ceiling of our room trying to escape at night and please, could we borrow some Polyfilla to hide it from the teachers?*" Brilliant, I don't think.'

There was a silence. Beaky looked like crying.

'If we can find where Bernard keeps his stuff, we can borrow a bit,' I said.

'That's stealing,' said Noel.

'We're already stealing the strips of wallpaper and the whitewash,' I said. 'If you're going to finicky about it we'll never get it done.'

'Not stealing isn't being finicky,' said Beaky. 'It's being decent.'

'I agree,' said Noel.

'Okay,' I said. 'How much is Polyfilla?'

'No idea,' said Noel.

'And *where* are we going to buy it?' I asked. 'Tomorrow is Sunday. We're on a Nature Reserve. I bet there aren't any shops in the middle of the sandhills selling Polyfilla on a Sunday.'

'I don't see why I should get into trouble,' said Beaky.

I didn't see that either, but I wasn't going to say so. If Norrie had been around it would have been all right. I'd have managed it with Norrie.

'Maybe if you just leave it, no one will notice,' said Beaky.

We looked at the trap door hole. It was *very* noticeable.

'If nobody notices it for long enough, maybe they won't remember who was in this room,' said Beaky. 'There must be dozens and dozens of School Trips using this place. They won't know which one.'

'Some hope!' said Noel, despondently.

'Leave it to the Espies,' I said.

'I suppose that means you're going to get Phyllis to help?' said Noel.

'We will hold Urgent Espie Consultations,' I said, trying to make a joke out of it, before they all started weeping or throwing themselves off cliffs or something.

'Remind her who cut the hole in our ceiling in the first place!' said Noel.

TEN

It was Sunday, so everybody had to go to church. Mum and Dad don't go to church, so we aren't used to it. We're agnostics.

'You shouldn't be in a Christian Church if you're not Christians,' said Waldo Milligan.

'You're supposed to be converting us to Christianity, Waldo,' I said. 'It's your Christian Duty. Maybe we'll get converted if we go in.'

We went in.

It was funny to see them all being dead quiet and polite.

I *think* I believe in God. I'm a sort of Positive Agnostic. My Dad says we should all live our lives as if there *is* a God, even if there isn't one.

They had a Collection Box and we all had to put money in, which wasn't funny, because we hadn't budgetted for it.

When we came out of Church Bernard was there in the landrover with Edwina and Norrie.

'He's right as rain!' Edwina told Trout.

Old Beaky went up and shook Norrie's hand and said 'I am very sorry, Norrie. It was an accident.'

'That's all right,' said Norrie.

'Good!' said Trout. 'No more fighting, eh?'

'You smash his face in for him Norrie, later,' said Sprout, when we were all on our way back to Murtagh House. Edwina must have got at Trout, because this time he didn't make us go in a crocodile.

'I'm glad that that is over,' Phyllis said to me. 'That is

eight churches I've collected now, and I'm not going to join any of them.'

'You can join the Fix-Our-Ceiling-Club first,' I said. 'You ought to be a Founder Member, considering you are the one who bust it.' I told her what we were going to do. 'Where do you think we could get the Polyfilla?' I asked.

'I don't,' she said. 'That's a silly idea anyway. Polyfilla and wallpaper! I can just see you and Norrie upside down in the bogs trying to peel wallpaper off with your penknives.'

'Okay!' I said. 'Okay! You're the Big Brain. You sort it out!'

'Toilet paper,' she said. 'Or newspaper. Thin rolls of it, rolled very tight, and pressed up into the gaps.'

'Don't be daft!' said Norrie. I was glad he was back anyway, because that meant one useful one on my side. Beaky and Noel were hopeless.

'We press the paper tightly into position, and then we put the whitewash stuff from the stable over it,' said Phyllis. 'I've seen Dad doing things like that round the windows.'

'With sellotape over the top,' I said. 'We fill the gaps round the trap door with rolled newspaper, and put a strip of sellotape on top to hold them in position, and then we whitewash over it.'

'Right,' said Phyllis.

'Great,' said Norrie. 'When are *you* doing it?'

'I'm not,' said Phyllis. 'It is your room. It will have to be done from *inside* your room, and the girls aren't allowed in the boys bit, so you and James and Noel and Beaky will have to do it.'

'That means me and you, Norrie,' I said.

'I wasn't even there!' Norrie groaned.

'Stop moaning, Norrie,' said Phyllis.

'When do we do it?' Norrie said.

'After we've been out,' said Phyllis. 'It's Last Night, and we've got to break out on the Last Night, so you'll have to fix the hole afterwards.'

'We'll have to have all the stuff up in our room, ready,' said Norrie.

'Newspaper, that's easy. I've got some sellotape,' I said. 'And we can use a cloth for a brush, if we can't find one. We'll put some of the whitewash in a bag and take it up to our room during the day. When the time comes we can mix it in the sink. Then we put the chair on the bed and climb up and whitewash. Easy-peasy!'

'Bet you get caught,' said Phyllis, not very helpfully.

'If *we* get caught, *you* get caught,' said Norrie.

'I don't want to be caught,' said Beaky. 'I haven't done anything to get caught for.'

'Then don't listen in to other people's conversations!' Norrie said.

Beaky cleared off. He was frightened of what Norrie might do to him, but we had already warned Norrie not to start anything, because this time we all thought Trout's threats were for real.

We all got back to the house and Trout said we could clear off to the beach for an hour or so while he and Edwina had coffee and a look at the papers, and then we could report back at the house for a Bird-Spotting Walk.

I nipped up to our room to get Beaky's rucksack to fill with whitewash powder. I didn't tell Beaky, because he mightn't have been too pleased.

There was a note on my bed. It had J. Espie on the front, and *Dear James, I love you forever. Lorna* inside, in Sprout's handwriting.

I screwed it up.
I didn't want anyone else seeing a thing like that.
Lorna came up to me when we were going to the beach.
She was all red.
'I never sent you that note, James,' she said.
'I know you never,' I said.
'Good,' she said.
Then she went off.
She was really embarassed.
I wonder who told her about it? I reckoned it must have been Sprout.

Norrie and I started to change, down in the bushes. We were going for a deep paddle because we had been told no swimming. So was everybody else.

Somebody shouted 'Fight! Fight!'
'Come on!' Norrie said.
We headed off for the fight.
They were over by the sea buckthorn. Somebody was in the buckthorn, but we didn't know who it was. Then Charlotte Wallace came up. She told us.

'Beaky Thornton has lost his clothes,' she said. 'It's disgusting.'

Old Carol gave a shriek! She came rushing back shouting. 'I saw his ...' and then she saw me and Norrie, and stopped.

She went scarlet, and went away.
Lorna came up to me. She was really angry. 'It was Buns and Sprout, James,' she said.

'Beaky's in the bushes with no clothes on, and I'm not going near there, no fear!' Charlotte said.

I went to see.
Old Beaky was in the bushes.
We couldn't see much of him, just his bare shoulders.

He was red in the face, and looked as if he was going to start crying.

'Where are they?' I said. I'd had enough of Buns and Sprout and Dennis.

'They've cleared off with Beaky's clothes,' said Waldo.

'How did they get them?'

'Beaky was getting changed, and Buns and Sprout grabbed his stuff, and his bathing costume and everything, and now old Beaky is stuck.'

'Come here, James,' Phyllis shouted.

I don't like her giving me orders.

'You come here,' I said.

'We *can't* come, with Beaky in the buff!' said Phyllis. 'You come here.'

She was with Lorna and Charlotte. I went back to them.

'Has he *really* got no clothes on?' said Lorna.

'It's them again,' I said. 'Sprout and Buns.'

'I'm fed up with them,' said Phyllis. 'There's going to be trouble, and Edwina told us if there was more trouble we would all be out, and what's more nobody would let the Memorial come back here ever again.'

'You'd better get him something to put on, James,' Lorna said.

I looked round for something.

'What about old Doris' cardy?' I said.

'He'd catch her warts!' Charlotte said.

'Shut up, Charlotte,' Lorna said.

'What warts?' I said.

'Old Doris has warts on her arms,' Phyllis said. 'They're not *dirty*. They came, all at once. She has to go to hospital and have them removed. They're just an infection. We're not supposed to know about them and you're *definitely* not supposed to know, and you *definitely* wouldn't know about them if Charlotte big mouth had kept her trap shut.'

'I'm not a big mouth,' said Charlotte.

'You shouldn't have told, Charlotte,' said Lorna.

'Anyway, we won't get Doris' cardigan off her,' said Phyllis. 'I wouldn't go around showing off warts, if it was me.'

In the end, I went back and got my towel. Norrie wouldn't give me his. He said Beaky had it coming to him.

'We're supposed to be on Beaky's side, Norrie,' I said.

'You are,' said Norrie. 'I'm not!'

It was up to me, then.

I went into the bushes, with the towel.

'Who is that?' Beaky said. He was crouching down behind a big clump.

'It's James,' I said. 'I've got you a towel.'

Beaky came out from behind the bush.

He looked dead funny.

He had no clothes on, only his BRIAN BRIAN BRIAN hat, positioned strategically.

'Give us it, then,' Beaky said, holding out his free hand.

'What have you got there, Beaky?' Waldo Milligan shouted. 'Crown Jewels?' He'd come up behind me.

'You shut up, Waldo,' I said. 'How would you like it?'

For a minute, I thought he was going to smash me one, for telling him to shut up, but he didn't.

'Buzz off, if you can't help,' I said, *and he did*!

I felt great.

I threw Beaky the towel. He put it round his middle.

'I'll get your clothes for you in a minute, Beaky,' I said.

I went to get the clothes.

Buns and Sprout and Dennis had his clothes. They were down on the beach.

'Give me those!' I said.

'Wait a minute,' Dennis said, slowly. 'Who do you think ...'

Buns moved, but I moved just before him. I grabbed the clothes.

I thought they were all going to pitch into me, but it didn't happen.

'I'll break your neck, Jimbo!' Dennis shouted.

Then the girls came. Charlotte and Phyllis and Lorna and Doris, and old Carol.

'You go and give Beaky his clothes, James,' Phyllis said. 'Dennis isn't going to touch you!'

'I'll kill him!' Dennis said.

He went to barge past Phyllis.

'Don't you touch him,' Carol said.

I wasn't sure which one she was talking to. Whether she meant Dennis wasn't to touch me, or Phyllis wasn't to touch Dennis. I don't reckon Phyllis could have done much about Dennis.

'You touch him, Dennis Ray, and I'll *tell*,' Carol said, blinking at Dennis through her glasses.

There was a dead silence.

'I'll *tell*,' Carol said.

Buns sniggered.

Dennis whirled round and swung his fist back to hit Buns and Phyllis grabbed his arm. He tried to swing forward, and she dragged along with it, then she fell over.

'I'll tell!' old Carol howled.

Dennis lowered his arm, and Phyllis let go.

Then Dennis called Carol a name and Carol started to cry.

'You've done enough for one day, Dennis Ray,' Phyllis said, and she got up and put her arm round Carol.

'You beetle off, Dennis Ray,' Lorna said.

I got Beaky his clothes, and he got dressed.
'Thanks, James,' he said.
We walked back up to the house.
Doris was there, waiting for us at the door.
'Where's Dennis?' I said.
'Don't know,' said Doris.
'What about old Carol?' I said.
'He should never have called her those things,' Doris said. 'She's in the back, with Phyllis. Don't you go near her, James Espie.'
'What did she do?' Beaky asked.
'Saved your skin!' I said.
'NOBODY is to tell Edwina and Trout anything,' Doris said. 'Do understand that, Brian Thornton?'
'Okay,' Beaky said.
I went off to the bog.
Norrie was in there.
'What did old Dennis do to Carol?' Norrie asked.
'I don't know,' I said.
'Yabba-dabba-do!' Norrie said. He was all excited.
'You dry up,' I said.
'What?'
'Old Carol was dead brave,' I said. 'She doesn't need you and your lot going on about whatever Dennis did to her.'
Norrie called old Carol the same name Dennis had called her.
'You say that again and I'll smash your face in,' I said.
Norrie went away.
I was glad he did.
I was half-frightened, and half-excited about everything. I'd had a go at Dennis and he'd backed off. I'd won but Dennis couldn't let me get away with it, not when it

had happened in front of everyone.

It was nearly lunch time.

I had the afternoon to get through, and tea time, and after tea-time, and then the Last Night ... all without Dennis getting me.

I wasn't going to make it.

The only way I could make it, was by getting Dennis.

I couldn't thump him, but maybe I could out-think him.

I stayed a long time in the bog, figuring out my tactics, and then I got ready to reappear.

My idea was okay, *if* it worked.

ELEVEN

We had our Bird-Spotting Walk after dinner, because Trout didn't get himself organised in time.

Bernard came with us. He knew a lot and was pretty interesting, when I bothered to listen. It was all very educational, and Beaky kept asking questions and showing off his bird book, but the best bit was Bernard's dog trying to lick Edwina's toes, and Edwina trying to let on that she didn't mind.

Edwina had sandals on. Her toes were sticking out, and I think the old dog liked the taste of her nail varnish. He kept sniffing after Edwina, and she kept dodging about. Maybe Edwina is scared of dogs. Anyway, it was interesting, and much more interesting than listening to Trout telling Beaky about what he had seen on some old Salt Marsh somewhere in the year dot.

Dennis and Sprout and Buns were all palsy-walsy again, but no one else bothered with them. The girls had ganged up on Carol's side, which served Dennis right.

We got back to the house, and the walk broke up. Then I threw a stick for Bernard's dog and the dog went plunging after it, straight into the flower beds. There were broken flowers everywhere.

'That's done it!' Norrie said.

'Not too clever!' Bernard said. 'Don't chuck things in there again.'

'Sorry,' I said.

Phyllis was in the recreation room, waiting for me.

'Going ahead with your Doing-Dennis plan?' she said.

I nodded.

'Best time to do it, I suppose,' she said, doubtfully. 'Most people are against Dennis now. They'll be on your side.'

'It will be all right if old Doris sticks to her lines,' I said.

I'd talked it all out with Phyllis, and we reckoned Doris was the best one to use, because she is cleverer than she looks, and she *definitely* doesn't like Dennis.

'They're coming,' Carol said. She'd been keeping cave for us in the hall.

Dennis and Buns and Sprout came in. Dennis and Sprout came *right* in, Buns stayed by the door. I suppose the idea was to stop me getting out.

'Here you are then, Jimbo!' Dennis said. 'Keeping out of my way?'

'No,' I said.

'I've one to even up with you,' he said.

'Don't you touch him, Dennis,' Phyllis said, making out that she was worried, when really Dennis was just playing to our script. So far, everything was just right.

'Why not?' said Dennis. 'Who's going to stop me?'

'Because you *can't* have a fight,' said Phyllis. 'If you have a fight, there will be a BIG row with Trout, and the Memorial will be stopped coming here forever.'

'Oh big deal!' said Dennis. 'I bet you worked that out between you!' He knew Phyllis was right, though. 'You're yellow, both of you.'

'I'm not yellow,' I said. 'I'd take on any two of you, Dennis Ray!'

'Listen to him!' said Sprout, inspecting his fist.

'Big talker,' said Buns.

'I'll take on any two of you, in a duel to the death!' I said.

'You can't fight two of them, James,' Phyllis said, coming in on cue.

'I'm not going to fight them,' I said. 'It's a duel.'

'Getting out of it!' scoffed Buns, who'd come away from the door.

'No, I'm not,' I said. 'I'm dead serious. I'm challenging any two of you to a duel. We can't have a fight, because Trout would go up the wall, but we can have a Contest to the Death at something else.'

'What?' said Dennis.

'What about pool?' I said, trying to make it sound casual. 'I'll take on two of you, in separate games. How about that?'

Everybody knows I am Pool Champion of the Memorial Lower School.

'Not likely,' said Dennis.

Old Doris came strolling in, as if she was looking for something. You'd never have known she was acting. She did it brilliantly! She should have got an Oscar.

'Oh well,' I said. 'If you are chicken ...'

'Who challenged who?' Dennis said.

'I challenged you lot,' I said. 'We can't fight because of Trout, but I am challenging you lot to a Pool Duel to the Death!'

Dennis winked at Buns and Sprout.

'You're *challenging* us?' he said.

'Yeh.'

'That means *we* get choice of weapons!' Dennis pulled his big idea out of the hat, like a rabbit.

'But there's two of you, and only one of me,' I said, trying to make it sound as if I'd only just caught up with them, when I was miles in front … at least, I *hoped* I was.

'That gives you twice the chance of beating us,' said Dennis. '*You* issued the challenge, so *we* get choice of weapons.'

'No dice!' I said. 'Pool or nothing.'

'You are yellow!' Buns said.

They all three started yapping at once.

'I'm not,' I said. 'I could beat you at Pool anyday.'

'But not at anything else, Jimbo!' said Dennis, screwing his face up to mine.

Then Phyllis came in. 'Let someone else choose the weapons,' she said. 'Me, for instance!'

'No way,' said Sprout. 'No way, Phyllis. You just want to stop Jessie James getting plugged.'

'Okay, let someone else choose, not me,' said Phyllis, backing off as if she was scared.

'Who?' said Dennis.

'Doris,' said Phyllis.

'No way!' said Sprout at once. 'Doris is your mate.'

'Keep Doris out of it,' I said. 'I choose Pool. I'm the one doing the challenging and I choose Pool.'

'Ha! Ha!' said Sprout. 'Likely we'd fall for that one, isn't it?'

'Doris?' said Phyllis.

'I think you are all silly, and I don't want anything to do with it,' Doris said.

Dennis looked at Buns and Sprout. They were all pretty sure they could mash me.

'Go on, Doris,' said Phyllis. 'Choose something for them to duel with. Otherwise they'll fight, and then we'll all be in trouble.'

'Choose Pool, Doris,' I said.

'I'm not choosing what you tell me, James,' Doris said. I

was afraid she was going to over do it, and muck everything up. 'I'm a neutral, and I choose ... *chess*!'

'Oh no,' I said. 'No way!'

'Oh *yes*,' said Dennis quickly. 'Doris is on *your* side, I reckon, and Doris chose chess. So you've nothing to complain about. You challenge two of us to a Chess Match ... to the death! We'll lick you!'

'I never said I'd stick by what Doris said,' I said. 'I challenged you to a game of Pool.'

'No, you didn't,' said Dennis. 'You challenged us to a duel, and because you issued the challenge we get choice of weapons, and you tried to nark about that and we got a neutral to choose and she chose chess, so you are stuck with it!'

'Chess,' said Doris. 'That's what I chose.'

'That's not fair. I can't play chess for toffee.'

'You back out, and everybody will say you're yellow!' said Sprout.

'You've got to play them, James,' said Phyllis. 'You let yourself in for it.'

'A proper Chess Match,' Buns said. 'Right. Two teams. There's the Chess Club Team, that's me and Dennis ...'

'What about me?' said Sprout, wanting in on the action.

'Toss for it,' said Dennis.

They tossed, and Sprout won.

'Our team is me and Dennis, and your team is J. Espie!' said Sprout. 'You get white on one board, and we get white on the other.'

'Is that the way you do a Chess Match?' I said, as if I'd never seen one.

'What about clocks?' said Buns.

'We won't need clocks,' said Dennis. 'Jimbo won't last long enough.'

'You're in the Chess Club,' I grumbled. 'You all play for the team.'

'Hard *chess*,' said Sprout.

'Okay,' I said. 'But it isn't fair.'

'We'll make it fair,' said Doris, coming in on cue. 'It's James against two opponents, is that right?'

'Yes?' said Dennis, smelling a rat.

'Well then,' said Doris. 'You aren't allowed to help each other!'

Dennis thought it was dead funny! 'We don't *need* to help each other!' he said. 'We can both smash him at chess anyday.'

'Okay,' said Phyllis, spotting the big opportunity. 'If that is what you reckon then it means you've *both* got to beat James to win. If he beats one of you, he wins.'

'Done!' said Dennis, confidently.

'Separate rooms, one game in each,' Doris said.

'Why?'

'To stop you two helping each other,' Doris said. 'That was my rule, and you agreed to it.'

'Okay,' said Dennis. 'Okay! If we win both games he is our slave forever, right?'

'Hey,' I said. 'It's not fair ...'

'We agreed to all your rules,' said Dennis. 'You agree to ours, right? This is going to be a proper Chess Match, held in two rooms, with Doris as umpire. Your team against our team. If we both beat you, you are our slave for ever. Right?'

'And if James beats one of you, both of you are his slaves forever!' Doris said.

'Yes, IF he does!' said Dennis.

'All right,' I said.

'What is the order of your team?' Phyllis asked Dennis,

and she pulled out a piece of paper. 'I'm going to write it down, so there won't be any funny business.'

This is what she wrote down:

CHESS CHALLENGE MATCH
Espie v The Chess Club
Board one: Dennis Ray (White) v J. Espie (Black)
Board Two: J. Espie (White) v Colin Wright (Black)

Colin Wright is Sprout's name, but everybody calls him Sprout.

'Right,' said Phyllis. 'We're putting one game in the Common Room and one game in here, and we'll have a referee for each game.'

'Who?'

'Ask Doris,' said Phyllis. 'She's the main referee.'

'Buns in one room, Phyllis in the other,' said Doris. 'That's one from each side, so there won't be any argument.'

It was *exactly* what we wanted, because it pinned Buns down. Walking about, he might have been a nuisance.

'Won't have much to do, only count Jimbo out!' said Dennis. 'When do we start?'

'Twenty minutes time,' I said. 'I have to go and check my defences!'

Then I got an old Chess Book there was in the Common Room. I sat down by the window and pretended to be mugging it up, just to get them windy.

'You won't learn how to play Chess in twenty minutes, Espie!' Sprout said.

'I'm just polishing up on theory,' I said.

'The theory is that we beat you!' said Sprout. 'That is going to be the practice, too!'

'You're interrupting my reading,' I said, and I went back

to the book.

Phyllis and Doris and Buns got everything set up, and lots of people heard about it and came in to see.

'You must be mad, James!' Norrie said, coming up to me.

'You can't play chess for toffee!' Noel said.

'What did you have to pick chess for?' Beaky said. 'You know they're *brilliant* at it!'

'They'll be bossing us all around for life!' said Noel, looking really miserable.

TWELVE

Dennis and I sat down, and shook hands over the chess pieces. We were short a rook, but Phyllis had nicked a salt cellar from the dining room, and we used it instead.

'Game starts *now*!' Phyllis said. She was our referee, and Buns was being referee at the other game in the recreation room, where I was playing Sprout.

Dennis moved one of his white pawns.

The pawn in front of the white king, two squares forward.

'Can he do that?' I asked Phyllis. 'Can he move it two squares?'

'Pawn's opening move, one *or* two squares,' said Dennis smugly, knowing he was right. He was looking pleased, because if I didn't know even the pawn moves he was sure to smash me.

'I thought he had to move the pawn in front of the Queen first,' I said, pretending I had been startled by his great move.

Phyllis frowned at me. She was afraid I was going to give it away. Maybe she was right, but Dennis didn't spot it.

'Do wrap up complaining, Espie,' he said. He must have thought I was really goofy.

'Ref?' I said.

'He can move any piece he wants to, James,' Phyllis said.

'I'd been expecting him to move the pawn in front of the Queen,' I said. Old Dennis was no dozer. He'd seen that the Chess book I'd been reading was called 'Queen's Pawn

Openings.' The Queen's Pawn is the one in front of the queen, and he wasn't taking any chances.

'I'll need to think about my move,' I said. 'I wasn't planning on that one.' I got up, and went into the recreation room, where I was playing the white pieces.

I made a move.

The pawn in front of the white king, two squares forward.

Sprout didn't waste time. He made his move.

The pawn in front of the black Queen's bishop, forward two squares.

'Sicilian Defence!' he told Buns.

'Yeh, I know,' said Buns.

'Can he do that?' I said earnestly to Buns.

'Yes, he can!' said Buns.

'I thought he would move something else,' I said, and I sat there looking worried. Then I got up, looked worried again, and went back into the other room.

I stood looking at the board.

'I've decided to play the Sicilian Defence!' I announced, and made my move.

The pawn in front of the black Queen's bishop forward two squares.

'That is the Sicilian Defence, isn't it?' I said innocently.

'Yeh, it is,' said Dennis. 'Where did you learn that?'

'Oh, I pick things up,' I said.

It was dead easy. I was playing black in one room against Dennis, and white in the other against Sprout. White moves first in every chess game, so I had only to let Dennis make his *white* move, and then go into the other room and make the same *white* move against Sprout. Then Sprout made his answering move, as *black*, and I walked back into the other room, and made the *same* move, as *black*, against Dennis.

They weren't playing me, they were playing each other, and I was walking from one room to the other making their moves for them. I got the idea from noughts and crosses. My Dad used to do it to Phyllis and me. If it worked for my Dad at noughts and crosses, I didn't see why it shouldn't work for me.

It worked B-R-I-L-L-I-A-N-T-L-Y.

Neither of them reckoned I could play, and they couldn't work out how I was making all these text book moves and setting traps and saying things like 'I've decided to play the Sicilian Defence.'

'Haven't you finished him off yet, Dennis?' Doris asked old Dennis meanly.

'Dry up,' Dennis said, moving his Queen.

Sprout and I had just taken his salt cellar rook only Sprout didn't know about it.

'Thinking about chucking it in yet?' Sprout said, when I went back into the other room.

'No way,' I said, and I made Dennis' move with the Queen.

'Good move!' said Buns, looking really astounded.

'Yeh,' I said. 'Not bad.'

'Result of the Chess Club Match against J. Espie,' Doris announced. 'Board One: Dennis Ray 1 J. Espie nil. Board Two: Colin Wright nil. J. Espie 1.'

Dennis had staged a great comeback after losing the salt cellar, and check mated Sprout down in the corner.

'The Chess Club are hereby declared to be J. Espie's slaves forever, as they have failed to win both matches against him, as boasted. All right?' said Doris.

Everybody cheered.

'How did he beat you?' Dennis demanded.

'I mucked it,' said Sprout miserably. 'I was a rook up and all!'

'You bet you mucked it!' said Dennis, fiercely.

'No talking in front of your Master, Slaves!' I said, and then I cleared off quickly, because I reckoned it wouldn't take them long to get mad with people like Carol and Doris standing round rubbing it in by saying they couldn't really believe the Chess Club had lost.

'They'll spot it!' I said.

'Doesn't matter if they do!' said Phyllis. 'You didn't break any rules. You played chess, and you beat *one* of them. That's exactly what you said you'd do. If they were too dumb to spot that they were playing each other, that's not your fault.'

'Tell that to Dennis when he recovers!' I said.

Lorna came up.

'Well done, James,' she said. 'You were really clever beating them. I didn't know you played chess.'

'He doesn't,' said Phyllis, and then she broke into giggles.

'What?' said Lorna.

'Tell her, James,' said Phyllis. 'She's all right. She's on your side.'

So I told Lorna.

'You never!' Lorna said.

'He did, did, did!' Phyllis chanted.

'Don't tell anyone, Lorna,' I said. 'I'm hoping they won't work it out until we've got home!'

'I wouldn't tell on you, James,' Lorna said.

She went off.

'You still coming out for Last Night?' Phyllis said.

'Yeh. I suppose so,' I said. We'd been to the tuck shop and we'd got Mars bars and coke and everything, hidden in our room.

'We'll have this sort of Feast, and then people can pair off, if they want to,' Phyllis said.

'Oh yeh,' I said.

'Lorna will be there,' Phyllis said. 'She told Carol she fancied you.'

'Did she?' I said. I had a feeling she was teasing me. Lorna would never have said that, would she?

'You'll have to wait and see what happens tonight, won't you?' said Phyllis, and she made her Oh-la-la face at me.

'You reckon?' I said.

'There's no accounting for taste, is there?' Phyllis said, and she went off grinning to herself as if she just said something very very funny.

THIRTEEN

We got out!

It was midnight, and there we were on the beach, Carol and Norrie and Doris and Noel and Phyllis and me.

And Lorna.

She had her duffle coat on, with the hood down, and her hair hanging down the back. She looked great, and straight away she was walking with me.

It was cold down on the beach. We could hear the water slipping in and out. There wasn't much light, apart from the distance glow of the red light that the Army used to guide their helicopters in to the camp at Kinleer.

We went right down to the water's edge, and walked along it.

'I don't think I will paddle,' Phyllis said. 'Brrr!'

'Let's have our Feast!' Doris said.

We went up into the wind blows, and found a secret one, where no one would find us.

'What about a fire?' Norrie said. 'We could get some wood, and have a fire.'

'No fear!' said Noel. 'Somebody might spot it.'

We had coke, and our Mars bars, and some biscuits Doris had brought, and peanuts, and a bag of crisps each that we all said we'd owe Phyllis for.

I gave Lorna my Mars bar, because she hadn't got one. She broke it in half, and gave me half back.

'Put that torch out, Norrie,' Carol said. Norrie had brought Beaky's flashlight. He had been using it to pour coke with ... so that he could *see* where to pour the coke, that is. Phyllis had brought some plastic cups.

'Yeh, put it out,' said Phyllis.

She was sitting beside Noel.

Noel looked really frightened!

Norrie put the torch out.

There was a sort of scuffling sound, and somebody went off round the side of the wind blow.

'Who was that?' Lorna whispered to me.

I reckoned it was Norrie, and old Carol.

'Coming?' I said.

'Yeh,' she said.

We kind of bumped into each other, getting up, and then she got hold of my hand. I gave her hand a squeeze.

Somebody giggled.

'Come on,' I whispered.

We found our own place, and sat down.

Lorna sort of leant against me.

'It's nice here,' she said.

'Yeh,' I said.

'I'm cold,' she said.

'Lorna?' I said.

She didn't say anything.

I put my hand up, and touched the side of her face, and her hair. It was soft.

'Lorna?' I said.

I got her nose. I meant to get her mouth, but it was her nose I got, first time.

'You taste of Mars bars!' she said.

We did it again. We were there, for ages.

'Okay! Okay! That's it! Lovebirds out! I'm freezing, and it's time we all went home!'

Somebody flashed the torch at us, winking it on and off.

'Clear off, Phyllis!' I said, caught in the blink of it.

'Everybody home!' said Phyllis. 'Doris and I are freezing!'

'*Can* it, Phyllis,' Norrie's voice sounded, from somewhere in the darkness.

'I'm freezing, too,' said Noel. He was standing beside Doris and Phyllis.

'*We* know that!' said Doris.

'That's *why* we're freezing!' said Phyllis, and they both started giggling.

'Shut up,' said Noel.

'Come on,' said Lorna.

I held onto her arm.

'Come *on*, James,' she said. 'There'll be plenty of other times.'

We all went back.

Doris and Noel and Phyllis went in front, and we came in the middle, and Norrie and Carol stayed at the back ... a *long* way back, some of the time. When we got to the stables, we had to wait for them to come.

'Boys in first!' I said. 'Just in case there's trouble waiting for us.'

I went up onto the stable roof, and along it to the fire escape ladder, up to the weather gauge platform, where I opened the door, and peered inside.

Then I gave the all clear.

Everybody got up easily enough, except old Doris. You should have heard the noise she made, getting across the top of the stable. I thought for sure that Trout would hear us, but he didn't.

We had to get back in through the trapdoor. We lowered Noel down first, then Norrie, and that left me.

I had no one to hold onto, so I had to dangle, and then I

dropped onto the bed with a big bang, and the chair fell over.

Dead silence.

We thought someone was bound to have heard.

Then ...

'Where's Beaky?' Noel said.

Old Beaky's bed was empty. He was supposed to be keeping cavey for us, but he'd beetled off.

'He's *told*!' Norrie said.

'No, he hasn't,' I said. 'He wouldn't.'

'That's right, he wouldn't,' Noel said.

'Maybe he's gone to the bog,' I said.

'Come on, Noel,' I said. 'Let's go and find Beaky.'

We reckoned Beaky must be in the bogs, so we tiptoed down to them. The light was on, and Beaky was in there.

He was over by the sink, rubbing at his eyes, and going 'Oh-oh-oh-oh!'

'Beaky?' I said.

He stopped oh-oh-ohing.

'My eyes!' he said. 'I've burned out my eyes!'

'What?' His eyes were red rimmed like a vampire's and all bloodshot.

He bent back over the sink, rubbing at them.

'You put that old stuff in my bag,' he said, between ohs.

'Whitewash!' I said.

'I got it in my eyes,' he said. 'I got it in my eyes and my eyes are hurting horribly and I can't see properly and ... oh-oh-oh.'

'Whitewash doesn't sting,' Noel said.

'*Limewash* does,' I said. 'It must have been limewash.'

'Limewash?'

'He's got limewash in his eyes!' I said. My Dad got it once, doing our back yard, and he had to go to the doctor.

I suppose I should have known, because Bernard had used it outside for the stables, but now it was too late.

Beaky had got lime in his eyes.

'Get Edwina, Noel,' I said.

'No!' Beaky moaned.

Noel went to get Edwina.

'Poor child!' she said, when she'd looked in Beaky's eyes. She had a lovely chinese wrap on over her nightie.

'Will he go blind, Miss?' I said. 'We didn't mean to blind him. We're were only fixing the ceiling ...'

'*Fixing the ceiling*?' Edwina said.

There was a silence.

'*I* made a hole in it, Miss,' I said. 'It was only *me*, mucking about.'

Noel didn't volunteer! He'd gone dead pale.

'*Will* Beaky go blind, Miss?' I said.

'No, James,' said Edwina. 'The silly boy won't go blind, but he is in for an uncomfortable night. Lime irritates the eyes, but he must have got plenty of water onto it quickly, so it won't be too bad. We'll stop at a chemists on the way home and fix him up.'

Then she went back to our room with us, and inspected the ceiling.

'Oh, James!' was all she said.

'We were going to fix it, Miss,' I said.

'I was in it too, Miss,' Norrie said.

There was a long silence.

'And me,' said Noel.

'But not Beaky,' I said quickly. 'Beaky had nothing to do with it. He couldn't stop us, that's all.'

Beaky was holding a wet flannel to his eyes. He sat there on his bed, mumbling about it hurting.

'*You* ...' Edwina said, and then she read us a long lecture that went on and on and on. She was furious, but she talked in a low, low voice, as if she didn't want anyone outside our room to hear her.

'You see the position this puts Mr Fisher in?' she said. (Mr Fisher is Trout's proper name, but nobody calls him it except teachers.) 'He bothers about you lot, he really does! He had to move heaven and earth to get this trip arranged, and you've been nothing but trouble on it from day one. One thing I can promise you: if the Head gets to hear about the way you have behaved we won't be able to arrange any more trips here, ever again. All Mr Fisher's good work undone. Trying to show a pack of little savages like you that there is another side to life. He doesn't deserve you, he really doesn't.'

'Yes, Miss,' we said.

'We'll see about this in the morning!' Edwina said, and she went off. She closed the door very quietly behind her, and tiptoed down the corridor.

'You could *almost* see through her wrap,' Norrie said.

'You're *despicable*!' Noel said. He was almost crying.

'*I* didn't do it!' said Norrie. 'It wasn't me who bust a hole in the ceiling, it was the Espie family!'

'You were glad enough to go Last Nighting,' I said.

'Yes, I was,' Norrie said. 'Yabba-dabba-do.'

I reckon the world could drop on Norrie's head, and he'd still be on about S-E-X.

We all got into bed.

We lay there in the darkness.

'You all right, Beakyman?' I said.

'Yeh,' Beaky said. At least he'd stopped moaning. Edwina said his eyes weren't *that* bad, and we were all relieved that he wasn't going to be blind for ever. He wasn't blind at all, really. He told Edwina he could see quite well, if it wasn't for the tears. They weren't real tears, just his eyes flushing themselves out, Edwina said.

I lay there thinking about the Last Night, and most of all thinking about Lorna.

It *wasn't* like Norrie said, or like waiting for Edwina to go swimming, or like the magazines and pictures, or the naked ladies on T.V.

She was much nicer.

Nothing had *happened*, the way Norrie meant, but inside me *everything* had happened, and no one could spoil that.

FOURTEEN

'Miss?' I said.

'Yes, James?'

'I'm really sorry, Miss,' I said.

We were down at the Arches Bridge, waiting for the bus to come and pick us up. It was the end of Trout's Big Weekend.

'So you should be, James!' Edwina said.

'Miss?' I said.

'Yes?' she said.

'What is going to happen, Miss?' I said.

I mean, nobody had said a *word*. We all thought we'd be getting into a terrible row, but instead things had just gone on as if nothing had happened, and we couldn't understand it.

She took a deep breath. 'Nothing James,' she said. 'But keep it under your hat!' Then she smiled at me.

'Nothing?'

'By private arangement with our good friend Bernard,' she said. 'He was *very* good about it. And let me tell you something, James Espie. I didn't do it for you!'

'Miss?' I said.

'I did it for *him*,' Edwina said, nodding toward Trout, who was busy giving Doris and Carol a lecture about sedge warblers because he thought he'd heard one.

'Miss?' I said. I was doing my 'Miss' bit again, but I couldn't help it. I really didn't understand. Was she in love with old Trout, or something?

'It was Mr Fisher's last trip with a school party, James,' she said. 'He wanted it to be a big success. Lots of other people didn't want it to happen at all, these things are difficult to arrange with the cuts. Mr Fisher practically had to go on his knees to the new Head to get it set up. I wasn't going to let anybody spoil it for him, not even you.'

I nodded.

'But don't you *ever, ever* let on what happened,' she said. 'There could have been an official complaint from the Trust, do you realise that? Damage to property! Add that on to rowdyism, fights, even one boy overnight in hospital. It would have looked as if ... as if Mr Fisher was too old to manage things properly. That's what the new Head would have said, anyway.'

'Mr Fisher's retiring,' I said.

'Give him something to retire with, James!' she said. 'Another one of his famous Trips to see his precious birds! That's what he's got now. Luckily he doesn't know half the things that went on, but I do!'

'We didn't mean it, Miss,' I said. 'Should we apologise to Mr Fisher? About the ceiling and everything I mean?'

'*No*!' she said, sharply. 'Don't you understand? He thinks it was a great weekend for everybody. If he knew about your ceiling, and the rest of the carry on, he would report it. That is the sort of man he is. So don't you ever tell him, James. Okay?'

'Yes, Miss,' I said.

'If you're very lucky, there might even be a trip next year,' she said. 'But if there is, *I'll* be in charge, and things will work differently!'

'Yes, Miss,' I said.

'*Yes*, James,' she said, and then she gave me a big smile. 'You've survived, haven't you?' She said.

'Miss?'

'And come out smiling as usual!' she said. 'You'll either be hanged or be Prime Minister, James Espie.'

'They've abolished hanging, Miss,' I said.

She groaned.

Then the bus came, and everybody started piling onto it.

'Bernard,' I said.

'Hi!' he said.

'Thanks about the ceiling, Bernard.' I said.

'Oh, that's okay,' he said. 'Don't do it again!'

'Thanks anyway,' I said.

Then I got on the bus.

'Well?' Phyllis said.

'It never happened,' I said. 'Get it? Edwina has covered up for us. Bernard's fixing the hole. But nobody is to tell, ever ever, do you understand?'

'Yes,' said Phyllis. Then she said: 'Teachers are funny, aren't they?'

'Yeh,' I said.

I went to sit beside Noel. I wanted to sit beside Lorna, but she was at the girls' end, with Charlotte and old Carol.

I couldn't sit with the girls, could I? I would have looked naff!

'We're going to get you, Espie!' Dennis said, poking me in the back.

Same old thing!

I sat looking down the bus, at the back of Lorna's head. She must have known I was doing it, because she turned round and looked.

Norrie poked his head between Noel and me, from the seat behind.

'Me in hospital, Edwina in her bathing suit, Beaky in the nude, Dennis getting done ...'